Ian Start is an art professor and poet, living and teaching in Providence, Rhode Island. After suffering an infection in his leg that left him disfigured and traumatized, he's been struggling to regain his emotional balance and find his voice again in his poetry.

It doesn't help when one of his students is murdered, and he's implicated. The chemistry is still there between Ian and Jake, who is his ex and the investigator, but being a suspect presents a barrier to their reunion.

Furthermore, Ian's injury left a massive scar, both physically and emotionally. He is not convinced anyone else should have to live with his disfigurement and his nightmares.

START TO FINISH

The Ian Start Mysteries

Pamela A. Williams

A NineStar Press Publication

www.ninestarpress.com

Start to Finish

Printed in the USA

Print ISBN: 978-1-64890-116-4

First Edition, October, 2020

Also available in eBook, ISBN: 978-1-64890-115-7

WARNING:
This book contains sexually explicit content, which may only be suitable for mature readers, graphic violence, and suicide.

For Rachel and Tony

Chapter One

As I hobbled to the door, I could see, through the leaded glass, a stout Black man in a dated tweed blazer. He was staring intently at my approach, which made me wish that I was dressed in more than a robe and flannel pajama bottoms. Opening the door, I saw that there was a second man, a few steps down, looking out toward the street. "Professor Ian Start?" said the man in front of me.

"Yes?" I said, tearing my gaze away from the familiar pale ginger head.

"I'm Detective Henry Ransom from the Providence Police Department. May we have a few minutes of your time?" At that point, the tawny head turned, and it was, as I knew it would be, Jake. Right on cue, Ransom said, "This is Detective Jake Quinn." Our eyes met and held. In the moment, I was delighted to see him. But in my moment of pleasure, I could see wariness and warning in his eyes, a slight shake of his head that clearly said *don't acknowledge.* I immediately assumed there were some gay identity issues at play and kept my trap shut. Everyone knew I was gay, but I was well aware of guilt by association.

"Yes, of course, come in. We were just having coffee. Can I get you a cup?" *Ever the perfect host, eh?* With no small amount of trepidation, I led them to the kitchen where Rita was sitting at my little table. It looks out over a small terracotta-tiled patio with a wildflower garden beyond, looking bleak and dead in the frigid morning with black stems and flower heads that hadn't been tended to before the winter frosts.

"Yeah, coffee would be good," said Detective Ransom. I raised my eyebrows at Jake, who merely nodded. I knew he took it black but inquired of both anyway. Rita introduced herself, and they all shook hands. *I* didn't get a handshake. I began to feel very nervous. My knuckles started to prickle.

Rita rents my street-level apartment. Short and trim, with crazy hair from an indeterminate ethnic background, she's my closest friend even if she is a social worker. I had an overload of social workers during the time I was in the hospital, all telling me how fucked up I was going to be when I got out. After that, I swore off them permanently, but Rita was the exception. Despite our connection, Rita was a little bit of an enigma; quiet as a whisper, I never heard music or a loud voice from her apartment, so it was hard to tell if she was home or not, and I never knew if she had company because she apparently didn't keep regular hours. But every Sunday morning without fail she'd be at my back door with croissants and hot chocolate and dressed in tight stretchy sportswear, perfectly comfortable with me in pajama bottoms and my faded silk robe. And that's how a Sunday morning found us, the second of January, a sunny, cold winter day, when we heard the knock at the front door.

"I'm going to head back downstairs, Ian. If you need anything, just call." And then she was gone. Cops can do that: clear a room instantly.

I poured two cups from the carafe and retrieved a carton of milk from the refrigerator for Ransom, letting him pour. "What's going on?" I asked.

Ransom spoke. Jake didn't say a word. "You are acquainted with a Thomas Wilson." Statement, not a question.

"He was a student of mine, yes." The answer to the nonquestion.

"Was?" Ransom asked, a hint of a challenge in the tone.

"Yes," I said warily. "He's taken his last drawing class. I teach drawing."

"When was the last time you saw him?" Again Ransom. Christ. This was bad. I was going to hear that Thomas was missing. Missing or hurt, or...no, not going there. My stomach roiled a little.

"What's going on?" I asked again. And in nearly a whisper. "What kind of detectives are you? Missing persons?" Yeah, like there are missing persons detectives. I was hoping for the best out of the only other option.

"Homicide," said Ransom. I sat down hard on the nearest chair. Ransom then asked again, "When was the last time you saw Thomas Wilson?"

No, I do not want to hear what's coming. "The last day of class. Um, the twelfth, I guess. He helped me load portfolios into my car. Are you telling me Thomas is dead?" Jake nodded but said nothing. "Are you sure? Sure it was Thomas? What happened? When?" They were wrong, had the wrong kid, were talking to the wrong instructor. I stared uncomprehendingly at Ransom. I couldn't meet Jake's eyes at all. I felt helpless. My knuckles began to itch, and I distractedly scratched at them.

*

The last class of the semester meant gathering student portfolios stuffed with the required drawings for the final review. The logistics of collecting these generally involved a student helping me tote the unwieldy load to my car. Some are classic black leather affairs with a handle, some are shallow aluminum boxes—I hate those; they are heavy and cumbersome—and some are homemade cardboard folders with a cutout handle and ties on the side. Those usually belong to students from middle-class families and scholarship students. Sometimes they're decorated with drawings but most often not, reflecting time constraints. Thomas had offered to help, even before I had made the request. I'd had him in most of my drawing classes. He was enormously talented, so I felt I could never teach him much, but he had to take the classes to progress up the academic tree in credits. We liked each other. He was a young gay man who had always been out, had the support of his middle-class working parents, and had not experienced the same homophobia that older generations had.

I was also aware he had a crush on me. I was not bothered by this realization. I'd crushed on many of my instructors. My straight colleagues talked about getting love notes, hints, come-ons all the time. Thomas had done none of those things. He was always polite, helpful, appropriate. But I could tell by how helpful he wanted to be, or the way his eyes lingered, and by the few times his adolescent body betrayed him. I'd wanted to tell him that it was normal. But I also remembered the humiliation of having my body unexpectedly show my desires.

"What's next for you, Thomas?" I'd asked. Although a painter, I was hired only to teach drawing classes, and Thomas had taken his last with me. He could have gone on to upper-level drawing, but he didn't need to. Thomas had wanted to be an illustrator and he was exceptional. I'd wanted him to pursue portraiture because of his uncanny ability to capture his subject's inner tone, but he was shyly uninterested.

"Oh, I'll work on my illustration and graphic design, I guess." He'd paused with a faint look of regret. "I'm kinda sorry I don't need any more drawing classes. I'm gonna miss y—them," he stuttered and then blushed.

"Well, I'll be around. Stop by and let me know how you're doing, will you?" I'd said as we finished loading the last of the artwork into the back seat of my Civic. He nodded. As I drove away, he offered a short wave. *I'd miss him too*, I'd thought at the time. He was a nice kid, genuine, warm, and bright, who didn't seem to have a lot of friends, and I'd felt quite protective of him.

I'd told the students I would have their portfolios graded in a week, and then they would have a week after that to retrieve them before the office staff was off for the winter break. If they weren't able to get them by then, they could pick them up starting the first week of January. With Christmas in the mix, portfolios often sat there until February. By the end of a semester, grading the work was not difficult. I knew where most of the students stood in terms of ability, effort, and passion for the subject. The hardest task was composing the short critique I enclosed with every collection. And if the student was in the upper-level classes, I'd attach a more thorough evaluation; after all, for many, it was their last drawing class. So I kind of had my work cut out for me for the next week. I remembered thinking that the task would keep my mind off the man who almost ran me down.

Only a few weeks before the end of the semester, on a day where the wind was blowing the rain sideways—I couldn't see much of anything, not even the big gray sedan turning right. I'd just entered the crosswalk, walking against the light, when the car skidded to a halt, and the driver blasted his horn. I froze, but between the swipes of his windshield wipers, I caught a glimpse of him. And he of me. When I finally walked on after he drove past, I'd thought at the time: *nah, couldn't be*. It was just a similar face. Lots of cute Irishmen in this part of the world. Nope, nope. But I knew it was him. Jake.

The raw, rainy Novembers of New England's South Coast are hard on my faulty leg, but I hobbled on, as fast as I could, to an early class. Even though I felt unsettled and agitated for the rest of the day, I taught my courses with as much attention as I could muster, despite that morning's shock and the rush of memories at seeing his face. I tried to concentrate on the utter delight I get out of helping young artists *see* what they're looking at, and learning what isn't there is as important as what is, so now I might sound like a professor—which I am: I teach drawing at Rhode Island School of Design. I teach students to begin a drawing by seeing the arrangement not by line but by space. Drawing classes, after all, are about depiction. The contrapuntal relationship between subject and negative space is the essence of representation. The form of a tricycle emerges from the shape of where the trike is not. Outlining is not the way to learn to draw, and nothing is learned until students can define an object by shadow, light, and space. When they internalize this concept, an instructor sees an artist in bud. It had been a typical day; the unrestrained hubbub of students filled the halls, and time was wasted by the tedium of repetitive and unnecessary paperwork created by an administration that had never done the work. But my edginess that day was unrelenting.

That evening in the comfort of home, naïvely hoping to avoid memories, I poured a double Lagavulin and gulped half of it immediately. I forced myself not to forgo dinner entirely, heated up leftover lamb stew, and shoveled it down while standing at the sink.

Then I headed up to my studio, intending to work on the third painting of a series of male nudes. They were stark: a myriad of flesh tones on unadorned backgrounds tending toward blues and greens, the depth coming from paint thickness and underpainting. I am an unabashed expressionist. I paint the way I experience, how I feel about what I see. My abstract figurative work has been described as "jewel-toned Willem de Kooning," or sometimes Egon Schiele. The "jewel-tone" descriptor is accurate, and while I like de Kooning's style, I don't particularly like his depiction of women. They seem to convey de Kooning's hostility toward them, more than anything, which I find too disturbing and negatively stereotypical. Some of my best friends are women. Egon Schiele, on the other hand, seems to see the injury in us all, even if his nudes provoke shudders. Regardless, I never appreciate my style being compared to others; it's unimaginative. My style's mine, critics ought to figure out a way to talk about it. I suppose all artists complain about being lumped together. I will only talk about my art in terms of paint, color, texture, and the elements. The remainder is internal. I put it out for viewers to have their own experience, draw their own conclusions, but my innards are nobody else's business.

But, anyway, that night, instead of picking up my favorite bristle brush, I settled back in my soft, ancient, paint-stained leather chair and stared at the beginnings of the nude and thought about Jake and about the time we'd first met. It was at a friend's art opening at a gallery near Rhode Island College where I had been teaching creative writing. I was standing in the gallery's loft space looking down at the exhibit when I spotted him. He was with a young redheaded woman whose arm was locked through his. He was handsome in a way that bordered on cute, but the expression on his face was too serious and thoughtful to be boyish. Tall, maybe two inches shorter than my six three, thick, pale reddish-blond hair that would curl if not cut short, high cheekbones in an angular face, a forehead in sculpted planes smooth as marble, with a lovely, full bottom lip, and a soft cleft in his chin. His face lit up when he laughed; his mouth open as if surprised, straight white top teeth visible, laugh lines folded around his mouth and eyes. Eyes a blue that was not like my ex-lover Arty's metallic shimmery blue, but a more intense, intent blue. I thought he was the most handsome man I'd ever seen. His gaze had caught mine, and I felt a stirring. There was something about how expressive his face was that made me think he was gay. *Mais, non, la jeune fille, oui?* Anyway, he'd turned away first, so there was my answer.

A half hour later though, I found him at my elbow sans said *"fille."* "I'm Jake Quinn," he said and held out his hand. "You're the poet Ian Start, aren't you?" I was flabbergasted. I'd published two small volumes and had featured in a few literary publications like *Two Penny Review*, and *New London Poets*, but I am about as far from well-known as a foot soldier in the movie *Ben Hur*. I seem to be more of a writer's writer, a gay one at that, and so another poet may have heard of me, but certainly no one at Barnes and Noble. Sales had been expectedly dismal. But that was ok. It is always flattering to see oneself in print, not to mention that a tenure-track professor must publish or perish.

"Yes, I am. How on earth did you hear of me?" I realized I wasn't letting go of his hand and chuckled a little as I finally withdrew mine. His grasp had been warm, dry, and intimate—or so I'd imagined.

He said, "I read a few poems of yours in a magazine." His voice was a clear baritone and fluid as glass. "They really resonated with me. Then I saw your books at the Harvard Book Store in Cambridge, down in the remainders section, so I bought one."

I have an ego. I was smitten. I asked him what brought him to the opening, and he said his sister was an art student at RISD, and they often go to art openings together.

"Sister? Ah, was that your sister I saw you with?" But what was I doing? Arty was in my life then, and I'd been a faithful lover. I'd never had a desire to stray. Only vaguely lonely when Arty wasn't around, I depended on my arts, writing and painting, to keep me busy, to keep me from thinking about what Arty was up to the evenings he was at his place in Manhattan.

"Mm-hmm," he said, "but she had a late date." And then he raised one pretty, tawny eyebrow... I took him home.

That was, what? Four, five years ago? In retrospect, those months were so uncomplicated, sublime. I was on my way to tenure and looking forward to a secure future. I was feeling confident, energetic, excited for...more. We were together from spring through the summer of that year. To have someone so available made me feel desired in a way I didn't feel with Arty. Jake, aside from the physical attraction, admired me, was impressed by me in a way Arty wasn't. It was flattering. Jake was funny and fun, open to new experiences, energetic and self-assured. And he was more adventurous in bed than Arty; he was not particular about positions. Arty only wanted to receive, and I missed the sensations of being entered that I'd discovered in my earlier sexual experiences. Jake had liked giving me those pleasures, taking control, and it was so erotic being taken, to cede control. But Arty was my first serious, long-term lover, and I was committed to him in a way that I couldn't well describe to Jake. I tried to be open and honest with him, but I knew that wasn't stopping the deepening of feelings on Jake's part. Mine too, maybe, but I only see that now.

*

Ransom was staring intently back. He had surprising hazel eyes, feline in their slight slant. "Who loaded Thomas's portfolio into your car, you or him?"

"I really don't know." I wanted to look away, but his stare felt like some kind of power struggle; it also seemed important that I maintain the eye lock. "How...how was he killed? When?" I'm not sure I wanted to know, but in the moment, I felt I owed it to Thomas to not shut him out in death. My mind raced through scenarios: Drugs? Didn't seem likely. Robbery? Christ, he was a student; no money there. Hate crime? Then my brain stalled, and I thought absolutely nothing. Jake was looking at my hands, watching the scratching, and I remembered an argument we'd had when we were seeing each other. He became unreasonably convinced that I scratched my knuckles when I was lying. The itch actually *is* some sort of reaction to my being nervous, or agitated, or, yes, when I'm lying. I'd accused him of being a perpetual cop; he'd continued to accuse me of lying (as my itch grew worse); it was a no-win argument, and I'd finally given up and said, "Whatever." Today, when I caught him watching my hands, I shoved them each into the opposing sleeves of my robe, kabuki-like.

Finally, Jake spoke the words I didn't want to hear. "It was a gunshot to the head, Ian, New Year's Eve." I thought it was kind of bullshit that he was the one to say it. I would rather it had been Ransom. I didn't want to associate those words about a lovely, vulnerable young man I'd cared about with Jake. I wanted to keep my image of Jake...well, untainted, maybe. It was then the threatening tears eased over and splattered onto my arm, making an alarmingly stark stain on the celadon silk of my robe. Jake stood. For a split second, I thought he was coming around the table to: What? Pat me on the back? Put an arm around my shoulders? Hold me? I snorted back a self-deprecating laugh. Jake plucked a couple of paper towels off the roll on the counter and handed them to me.

"May I ask where you were around eleven that night, Professor Start?" Ransom spoke in a quiet smoker's voice. It was an even tenor, not monotone or emotionless, but jaded, perhaps, as if he'd heard it all.

I felt the heat rising in my neck and was embarrassed by the inevitable blush I knew I sported. It looks like a runaway rash. The reddening starts at my neck and runs like estuaries up my face in unattractive rivulets. If I looked guilty of anything, it was of the ugly show, even though it was from indignation and disbelief at the meaning behind the question. But Ransom wouldn't know that. "I was here, in my studio, all night." Now my knuckles were at a full-blown burn.

"Anyone see you here? Maybe you got a phone call? Made a call? Sent an email? It was the holidays, so did you talk to family or friends, maybe on New Year's Eve?" Ransom again. I wondered if there was some agreement that he would be doing all the talking except to deliver the really shitty lines?

"I was painting. I tend to shut the world off when I'm in my studio. No one called. I checked my phones the next morning." By shutting the world out, I mean that I put music on that I eventually don't hear and fall entirely into the painting. Often, when I put my paint-laden brush to a canvas, I fall into an abyss and results can be horribly beautiful. The finished work often terrifies me.

"Had Thomas ever visited you here, at your home?" Ransom continued. Some faculty had parties or gatherings with students, but I am somewhat introverted and never had students over. Call me rigid or old fashioned, but while I would chat with students in the coffee shops around town if I saw them, I thought it was always best to keep clear boundaries.

"No. I don't have students here. Ever."

"Ever meet with Thomas off-campus anywhere? His apartment, maybe?" Ransom's questions, let alone his stare, were getting annoying, to say the least. I sipped at my coffee, gaining a few seconds to corral my tendency toward sarcasm and snark. But then I started overthinking that move and wondered if they thought I was delaying answering to craft a lie.

"No. Of course not." I'd see him at coffee shops sometimes and perhaps chat for a few minutes, but that was it. I would have long conversations with him at school in the art office, but I felt disinclined to share.

"You left graded artwork folders, portfolios, for your students at your school office last month, right?" I nodded. "Do you remember what day that was, the time?"

"I think it must have been the eighteenth. Before Christmas anyway. In the morning, late morning. Jennifer, the art department's student assistant, helped me unload them. She might remember the time."

"And you are sure you never met with Thomas outside of RISD, never went to dinner or a movie, socialized?" Huh. Ransom had a way of saying a whole bunch in one word, and I knew exactly what he meant by "socialized" despite the neutral, guileless way he spoke.

"What's going on here? Why these questions?" This time, I did not bother to hide my increasing annoyance.

"Professor Start, there were some...indications in Thomas's apartment that imply there might have been something more than just a teacher/student relationship between you and him. Would you like to comment on that?" Ransom was exceedingly polite in everything he said or asked, and I thought the effect was worse than some hardboiled type getting in my face. At least then I'd have a better reason for punching him in the throat.

I didn't punch him in the throat. Instead, I stood, my mouth opening and closing like a landed trout. I looked back and forth between Ransom and Jake, mentally willing the morning to rewind itself. Finally, my focus fell on Jake and stayed. He met mine for a long second, his navy eyes cool. I never thought they could be anything but warm until now. He looked away. I plopped down again, feeling utterly defeated, and it had nothing to do with the near accusation. It had more to do with Jake's iciness.

I'd imagined Jake here in my home with me countless times after Arty left. Now here he was, and I was afraid of him. I felt abandoned. Guilty, but of nothing, and there was no one but me to stand and defend. The current span of circumstances underscored the feeling I'd had for a long time that there was a hole in my heart. I seem to have chances, and this great big black undefinable abyss that is my life just sucks possibilities, hope, want, into some unknowable, unfathomable deep sea. The entire situation felt ominous from fore to aft.

"Well, that's just bullshit," I said tightly. "I don't know where these 'indications' came from, but they are categorically untrue." Categorically? Christ. I sounded like some first-year law student. Worse, I sounded way too strident. "What are these indications, anyway?"

"No offense, Professor Start, but we aren't ready to share a lot of details yet. I'm sure you understand," Ransom said. No, I really didn't understand, but again, I declined to say so.

Finally, Jake spoke. His tone reminded me that he was not Jake, my erstwhile lover, but a cop. And his face was expressionless. I'd never seen Jake without an emotion playing across his face. I didn't like it.

"Did Thomas ever talk to you about his personal life? Lovers, friends, hookups, people he hung out with?"

"No. Not much," I stated tonelessly.

"Did he talk about any trouble he was having with anyone: boyfriends, employers, instructors?"

"No," I responded again, matching his lack of emotion. I was looking him in the eye, and there was nothing. Not a look of familiarity, regret, sorrow. Nothing but a vague wariness. As though he were talking to, looking at, my doppelganger, not me.

"Ever tell you that he'd been injured, by anyone, maybe someone he was having sex with?"

"No, never." *What was that about?* I wanted to know more, but not from them.

They asked a few more questions about my private and RISD email, shook my hand, and left, stating they would undoubtedly be back. I rubbed my hands up and down my face, wiping away leftover tears, trying to start some circulation somewhere. But I was suddenly and thoroughly exhausted. I wanted sleep, and for sleep not to end. I wanted my cat and my downy cocoon. I wanted comfort. Truth be told, I would have wanted the comfort to come from Jake. But I knew he was on the wrong side. Now he was someone to be feared. I wondered what he'd tell Ransom about my itching. Panic hit me like a cyclone.

Chapter Two

Christmas this year, had been a nonholiday for me. I had indeed been in my studio almost nonstop from Christmas Eve until New Year's Day. Ransom had asked me if I had an alibi. He'd asked if I'd talked to anyone, even family. I have no family to speak of. Well, I have my very problematic mother, to whom I talk reluctantly, and a sister in DC, to whom I don't speak at all. She's nine years older than me; we were never close. I was always aware that I made her uncomfortable. When I officially came out in my teens, she'd been married to a conservative Christian minister for two years. Yes sir, that was pretty much that. I don't know if her decision to completely reject me was hers or her husband's. I didn't know her that well to begin with. At a rare family dinner, shortly after my announcement, my sister handed me a list of conversion-therapy clinics, explaining they were of good repute, and her husband could help me get into the one of my choice, that I didn't have to live like this, that I could be happy, meaning straight, I supposed. I snorted back a laugh, thanked her, took the paper and lit it on fire from one of the candles and tossed it into the fireplace. My father guffawed, my mother cleared her throat and said, "That's enough of that, Theresa."

My parents were fine with my "preference," as they called it—as if it were changeable; this year I have a preference for...blue. Easy. Complete acceptance. But that didn't mean I had anyone to actually talk to about being gay, about dating, about love, sex. I think my life as a gay boy was viewed by my parents as something they were not qualified to help me with. As though my brand of love was a different beast.

My British-born father was killed in a car accident when I was twenty-two. I was devastated and angry and hated myself for wishing it had been my mother. He had been my strongest ally, my friend, my reason for choosing art and literature, but not a confidant. He was an architect who'd wished he was an artist. We would spend hours in his studio at a marvelous gigantic tilting drafting table, he with his rolls of specs, me with my cray-pas and paper. He saw something in me that no one else had, I think. He was the one who stuck my childish drawings on refrigerators, encouraging me to pursue art. Two years after he died, Mother remarried a very rich asshole from Connecticut and moved from our home in Manhattan to Danbury.

My mother had read me poetry as often as stories, but never really encouraged my writing, never much praised it, despite my unrelenting efforts to win her approval. I think her motive for her restraint in praise was to save me from a swollen head. She must have equated self-esteem, pride in one's self, with pridefulness. My childhood with her was a cycle of hope and disappointment. There was this tease about her; maternal love was held aloft like a donkey with a carrot hung before him, walking perpetually toward the unattainable. I did not realize what a burden my mother's presence was until I left home for college. While my father was an easygoing, laid-back sort of guy, my mother was a nervous, rigidly contained, snob. I always wondered why my father loved her, which he plainly did. He was affectionate and considerate of her, while she was never entirely comfortable with that. She'd tolerate his physical affection with an air of resignation and then mumble about his lack of financial acumen. We were by no means lacking, quite the opposite, but my mother was never wholly satisfied with anything or anyone, including herself, I imagine. While she always wanted the best for me, even though it was often what *she* wanted rather than what I wanted, it's painful to be around her. So holidays are spent with friends or on my own.

My friends understand me, so they don't get annoyed or worried about my decisions to partake or not, but acquaintances do annoy me. They assume that I am some poor, nearly forty-year-old urchin pining for a pseudo-family to take him in. Every year around this time I am bombarded by the same old faculty and faculty spouses, inviting me to their house for Christmas Eve dinner, or Thanksgiving, or Easter, or Passover or, or, or. I cannot seem to convince them I am fine. And this winter break I'd had a concept for a painting. I'd sequestered myself in my studio, with my little half kitchen and plenty of scotch, and painted.

When I'd gotten the settlement money after my injury, I bought a brownstone on College Hill very near Brown and RISD. It was four stories. When I'd bought it, each floor had been an apartment. I left the ground level as a separate unit (it had a street-level entrance), rehabbed it as a decent apartment, and lived there as the rest of the flats were converted back into a single living space. It's far bigger than I need, but I fell in love with the old architecture, hardwood floors, elegant trim work, and the way the living space flowed. The front room, with its angular oriel window, looks down on Benefit Street. It opens to the dining room in the middle, then partially opens to the kitchen at the back. The entire first floor has an airy, spacious feel. There is a narrow nook on the right that hides a tiny half bath and my laundry. Three bedrooms and two baths are on the next floor up, and my studio is on the topmost level at the back. The room has exposures on all but the east side. My study, where I write, yeah, *used* to write, is at the front of the top floor, having all but the west exposure. The studio/den space is really what sold me, indeed not the price, which definitely gave me agita and still, from time to time, causes feelings of decadence and overindulgence. Fredrick reminded me I could afford it, and I deserved it. *Tsuh, buy it, you dolt.*

If it hadn't been for Arty, my partner at the time, I wouldn't have what I have now. Arty had been the one to insist on a lawyer two days after I'd been admitted to the hospital. He is the head librarian for a prestigious contract-law firm in Midtown Manhattan. While his firm didn't specialize in personal injury law, his friendship with one of the partners of his firm enabled us to retain a white-shoe Fifth Avenue law firm who did: Franklin, Burstein and Sachler LLP. They were sharks and perpetually hungry. Suing the mega franchise would be another famous name in a long list of successes for them. It took almost a year, but the settlement was preposterous; enough to set me up for life, and enough for another life too. I'll always be thankful to Arty for that. But it took a while for me to get to the gratitude.

Arty and I did not make it to the end of the legal wrangling. By the time the money came through, I knew that the sight of the scar (scar! what a tame, polite word for what was left) turned Arty off physically. I saw that he tried, but the harder he tried, the uglier I became to myself. I became depressed and remote, and he didn't know what to do with me, how to help bring me back. I think that in some unacknowledged way he had lost what he most valued in me, which was his ideal of perfection. I knew that I was attractive in a moody, brooding way: tall and slender, my face all angles and deep-set eyes. My body, toned from running, was the type he considered beautiful. Ironically, I was never particular about my looks. I knew what they could get me, but what I ultimately struggled with was how it interfered with what *I* needed; Arty liked his men pretty. Pretty and perfect and not fucked-up.

Arty was a short, wiry guy with perpetually thinning hair which he'd kept closely shaved. He had sparkling pale-blue eyes behind wire-framed glasses, a wickedly bookish and sophisticated sense of humor, and a delicious smile, which he engaged often. He was a Proustian, which both amazed and bored me as I never got past the first ten pages of *Swann's Way*, despite having picked it up at least ten times during the time we were together, which was— how funny!—ten years. *So many tens*. I loved him. After I moved to Providence, we managed the three-hour distance by doing alternate weekends. He had a prime postage stamp of a rent-controlled apartment in Greenwich Village, which he would never give up, well, at least not for me, and I, an unmemorable apartment in East Providence. Arty could be brilliantly silly. He was a kind man, never catty or vicious. He was a sensitive lover, and I knew he'd cared for me. I was his, as they say now, primary partner, but I knew I was not his only, so I took what I could get. At the time, it didn't feel like settling. Today, it does.

The beginning of the end of us started so innocuously. A little cut on my upper thigh from a sharp, bent piece of metal in a doorjamb at a Starbucks in the Village. After mentioning it to the manager, who stated that, yeah, I wasn't the first, and he'd been meaning to get it fixed, I thought nothing of it. I washed it off when I got home, slapped a bandage on it and continued on my way. As far as I noticed, it was healing normally. Then about four days later, it started to hurt. And by hurt, I mean it felt like a hot poker in the side of my ass, but deep inside. The cut itself didn't look too bad. It was a Thursday when the pain started. I decided that if it was still as painful on Monday, I'd go to an urgent care clinic. And then I got what I thought was the flu. By Sunday evening, I was in Rhode Island Hospital—in surgery. I'd collapsed at lunch, feverish, ill, unable to put weight on that leg. The next three weeks were spent in and out of surgery as doctors chased the flesh-eating infection up my thigh into my left glute gouging and cutting away necrotizing muscle and flesh, debriding, debriding, debriding. Then the infection laughed and ran the other way down my thigh and into my calf before it got bored and quit. I lived. My left leg looked like shit. I couldn't bear the sight of it. The entire time much of the injury had to be left nearly open, with only a light dressing. So counterintuitive, yes? We are supposed to cover wounds. It had been a gagging, putrid site, sight, and smell. Even the dressing changes were excruciating despite attempts at local numbing. At times they had to use general anesthesia.

My mother had made three visits. Each time, her nose, under her paper mask, had risen further and further toward her eyes, presumably dragging her upper lip with it, until I couldn't stand that sight either and had shouted,

"Christ, mother, smear a little Vicks under your nose! That's what cops do around rotting flesh, a DB." She'd lifted one flawlessly waxed eyebrow and asked what a DB was. I told her. And I told her not to come back. She didn't. Dead body. Well, but I wasn't wholly dead, was I? Maybe a sixteenth dead? A thirty-second? Sixty-fourth? How do you measure spirit?

DB. I'd learned that term from Jake. One spring before the injury, when Arty was unusually enthralled with a paramour and wasn't around much, Jake and I had the affair. He was, at the time, a cop in Brockton, Massachusetts, intent on becoming a homicide detective, and I'd learned a lot of cop-speak. But late that summer Arty had waltzed back in, and Jake had demurred, gracefully, if wistfully.

The horror of the open wound and the pain haunts me still. In dreams, it can come in the Halloween splendor of gory half-skeletonized men. Awake, odd things relating even obliquely to pain or injury can bring a dizzying photo-realistic reliving, or for no reason, I can find myself gasping for breath, sweaty and scared. I intentionally avoid memories. Remembering certain parts of the ordeal can make me queasy, like when the infection ended, and the skin grafts started. Although I could no longer see bone, the grafts looked alien. Flesh and muscle and bone were at least me. An awful, inner me, but me. The grafts were judderingly foreign. And as they started to come to life, they seemed to swell and lay puffed and eerily rosy atop the wound. No match to my pale, *porcelain complexion* as Arty called it. The first grafts failed. They tried a second with a different technique. Much of it failed, too, as did much of the third. I finally told them to stop. To let it just heal as it was. I wanted to go home, but I was informed that the wound would heal more slowly, painfully, without them. Eventually, most took, but there was little cosmetic benefit. The cleft, the valley, the granulated canyon, the leg, which once held a runner's muscle, had me dependent on a cane and was often unreliable. But, *bien sur*, I am alive! And if one more person reminds me of the odds of surviving necrotic fasciitis, I shall surely bash them over the head with my ugly black cane. Because of this abomination, I live alone. Well, my cat doesn't mind it. She's too polite to stare at it anyway.

One evening, shortly after I'd seen Jake in Providence, the day he'd almost run me down, I was sitting in the amber of the waning light in my studio, and I thought about calling him. I even opened my cell phone and scrolled to his name but froze as the memory of an encounter that happened a year or so after I'd gotten out of the hospital reared its spiky head. I'd gone to a popular gay bar with my friend Fredrick. It was a comfortable place for a drink and if you got there early, not too much of a meat market. A nice-looking man, probably in his midforties sat at the end of the bar around the L so that we were half facing each other. He bought Fredrick and me our next round, and when we looked over to acknowledge the drinks, his eyes were locked on mine.

"Jesus, man, go for it. He's gorgeous," Fredrick whispered. I had not been with anyone since Arty and was convinced that the gruesome vision that was my leg was going to be a permanent showstopper. Fredrick and other friends had been adamant that it wouldn't be. I'd begun to believe them, and I thought maybe I was ready to try. But how does one manage this conundrum? Was this similar to having an infectious disease? Do you tell a potential partner immediately? Do you get to know each other and hope for a connection before you drop the bomb and/or the pants? Do you say nothing and just tread water? I held my breath and jumped. I smiled back.

His name was Charles. We met for a few dinners before he invited me back to his house. There were no fireworks, but there had been a spark I thought we could, perhaps, fuel. The idea of sex with him was attractive. He was built like a swimmer with broad shoulders and narrow hips. He had latte skin and a British accent. Yep. Sex was sounding fine. I answered his questions about my limp without detail. An injury involving some muscle. He didn't pursue it.

After drinks, he suggested the bedroom, and I followed him down a short hall. He was not much of a kisser; some men aren't. Disappointing but, whatever. After pulling our shirts off he started to unbelt my trousers. I was definitely nervous and nearly stopped him. But to tell the truth, I had not had sex since Arty and was hungry. I suggested that he get in bed, and I'd follow. He gave me an odd look but did it. I walked around to the other side keeping my right side to him, slid out of my trousers and boxers, slipped under the sheets, and rolled quickly onto my left side. Maybe I could orchestrate this without...

Charles was clearly a top. After some mutual groping and stroking, both of us clearly aroused, he rolled me, stomach down. Uh oh. His cock was pleasantly nestled in the crack of my ass, and his hand stroked down my left side abruptly stopping at the bumpy divot in my left cheek. Looking down along my side, he saw it. "Fucking Christ!" The words still echo, the horror-stricken tone I'd feared. He sat up abruptly and asked what had happened,

"Attacked by a shark?" He tried to sound flippant, but he was no longer aroused, and there was a thin film of sweat on his upper lip. He did not lie back down. After a mumbled apology and a lame "Maybe we should slow this down, meet a few more times for dinner," I dressed quickly and made my escape. My face blazed in humiliation the entire way home. He hadn't called again. I never called him.

Later, Fredrick had said, "What an asshole. Some queers are such shits."

I'd put the phone away.

Chapter Three

After Ransom and Jake left, Rita found me on my knees, shaking in a cold sweat, in the small bathroom off the kitchen. I'd heard her calling from the back door in the midst of vomiting the meager contents of my stomach, but I just couldn't be arsed to answer.

"Jesus, Ian, are you okay? What is it? What's happened? What did those guys want?" I couldn't lift my head. I felt so good with my head nestled in my arm, resting on the seat of the toilet. I wanted to just stay there. I shook my head so she'd stop talking. I needed a minute.

"I'm okay, Rita. Wait in the living room, huh?" I know I sounded sharp, but I didn't want her there. She patted my damp shoulder and backed out, leaving me to heave once more before I felt my stomach settle. I stood at the sink and splashed cold water over my face and the back of my neck. I took a swig, swished and spat to wash out the taste. Calmer, I assessed myself in the little mirror; I wasn't mad at Rita, I was just angry. Angry that Thomas was dead, angry that Jake popped up, angry that I felt something. How comfortable it had been these last few years not to feel anything. Part of me wanted to maintain that numbness, nurture it. I shuffled pathetically into the living room.

"What's going on, Ian?" Rita sounded less worried and more insistent.

"Look, I don't think it's a big deal. Well, it is, because a student is dead, was killed, actually. And that was Jake." I sat next to her on my overstuffed leather couch, resting my jaw in my hands, my elbows on my knees. She was curled up catlike with Clio, my Siamese, who was sitting on the back of the couch getting her chin scratched. She eyed me suspiciously. Actually, they both did.

"That was Jake? I wouldn't have thought you went for older, fat, balding guys." She could do deadpan, my Rita.

"Yeah, funny." I sighed, not sure I wanted to relive the last hour.

"Who was killed, Ian? One of your students?"

"Yeah. A boy named Thomas. A nice young boy named Thomas..." I sat back, raking my fingers through my sweat-dampened hair. "They said they had something that implies that I was having a...an...well, an affair with him, I guess. They wouldn't give me details. And then that goddam Jake was there and the way he looked at me. I knew I shouldn't say anything to that other cop about us knowing each other. But he looked at me like he maybe thought I could do that. Do something like that. Kill someone." Another wave of nausea hit me, and I sat forward again, swallowing back the bile. Rita jumped up and headed to the kitchen, I could hear the tap running. What was all this nausea about, really? Was it about Jake, or about Thomas, or being a suspect in a murder? Regardless, the whole scenario did not bode well for happy endings, did it? What kind of ass was I? This nice, talented, friendly kid had been shot in the head. How could I even think about Jake? Sometimes *I'm* a complete shit.

Rita came back with a glass of water and sat on the coffee table across from me. "Start from the top."

I sipped cautiously at the cool water until I knew I could keep it down and then told her the whole story start to finish, including how I knew Thomas, how we had talked from time to time. In the art office. Which was shared by other adjunct instructors. Never in private. Great, now I feel compelled to defend myself to my best friend.

"Well, so, that doesn't sound so damning, Ian. I think the cops will investigate and clear this up, don't you? They'll find who did this and then you can call your Jake." Rita sounded so sure of this fantasy outcome, but she hadn't seen his face.

"Yeah, sure, of course." I stood. I was dismissing her rather abruptly, but suddenly I just needed to be alone. She stood, too, and we headed toward the back door. "I'll call you later, Rita. Thanks for, well, thanks." I pulled her into a hug. She wrapped her short arms around me and squeezed. She was the only person I could get genuine hugs from, and they were always warm, so warm.

Christ. What I was feeling was too complicated. I needed to just focus on what was important; Thomas had been murdered. I wondered what his parents were going through. He'd talked about them. Not a lot, but if I'd ask him, he'd respond with a short answer that made them sound like regular kind folk, leading a regular kind of life. It made me contemplate grief briefly, wonder about how my mother grieved my father. She never showed much emotion in front of us when he died, but there was a dimming in her eyes that never quite left. I grieved my father by staying away from my mother and drinking, and otherwise avoiding unpleasant emotions.

I headed back to my couch, a headache just starting in the upper left quadrant. If I swallowed enough ibuprofen, I might be able to ward it off. I detoured to the bathroom and snagged four tablets. I washed them down with the water Rita'd left me in the living room and lay down. So, apparently, I was under suspicion of murder for someone I'd cared about. I felt utterly, painfully in control of nothing. I turned my face into the leather of my sofa, pulling my alpaca throw haphazardly over me. There was a vague animal smell coming from my surroundings—the leather, the wool—that was primal, comforting, simple. I dropped off.

I awoke with a gasp, to banging at the front door. It was already dark. I must have slept all afternoon. I'd been having another nightmare...

I was standing with my back dangerously close to the edge of a high cliff abutting the sea. It was night, but full of color. Deep Prussian blues and dark emerald greens, an unearthly ocean-colored heath covering surrounding hillocks. I could feel the damp wind on my leg, smell a briny odor. I looked down at my detested limb, once again raw and exposed, the gory reds aglow in complementary hues to the surrounding blue-greens. In the dream, I knew that this horror was now my terrible leg's permanent condition, open and bloody, subject to the elements. I had nothing on but my robe, which was blown back, making my leg, my nudity, visible to all. As I stared at it, mortified, I heard someone in front of me laughing: a cruel, mocking laugh. I did not want to look up. The pain of hearing Arty's once-beloved laugh so twisted and vicious told me I only had to step back.

Jake was calling my name at the side window. He was bent back precariously from the top few steps of the entry, peeking through the side window into my living room. He must have seen me there in the dim light from the foyer chandelier. I sat up. My left leg was freezing, I must have kicked the throw off. The knocking continued as I realized that I was still wearing only my pajama bottoms and robe. Jesus, he'll think I'm some kind of decrepit, depressed, washed-up writer, a has-been, a nobody. Maybe I was. I had been feeling so empty lately. Was it only this morning that they'd told me what happened? Time is a terrible mate in its fickleness.

I pulled my robe around me, retied it, ran my fingers through my hair, and shambled stiffly to the door.

"I can't be here," said Jake, looking over his shoulder.

I swept my arm in a horizontal arc. "And yet, here you are." Probably not the time for sarcastic repartee. I tried to moderate the tone a bit. "Come in, Jake. Sorry, come in."

He followed me into the darkened front room and stood as I drew the blinds and turned on lamps. The deep cadmium-yellow walls glowed gold and warm and somewhat comforting. "Sit, please. Do you want a beer or a scotch? You used to like my Lagavulin." I did not add that I often thought of him when I drank it.

"Yeah, I remember. Nah, I'll just have a beer, thanks." He sat on the edge of the nearest chair, his arms resting on his thighs, looking down, avoiding my eyes. So handsome. Tonight he had a little golden red scruff on his chin that sparkled in the lamplight. It looked sexy, enticing. Right. As I walked back to the kitchen, I was overly conscious of my limp and tried to lessen it by walking slower. Glancing back, I caught him curiously eyeing my leg. I shrugged, gave up the affectation, and hurried for the beer.

I brought him a Peroni and, with my scotch, sat across from him on the sofa, not conscious of pulling the throw over my leg. I gathered this wasn't an official visit, but it didn't really feel like anything social either. I said simply, "It's nice to see you, Jake."

Jake cocked his head like a curious puppy, and I remembered that. Memories of Jake and me having sex in my apartment in East Providence flooded me, and I felt my balls tighten a little. But the recollection that Jake was here as a result of a murder he thought me guilty of chilled me, and the heat vanished in an instant.

"Yeah. You too," he said sounding a little reluctant. Silence then, and I waited for Jake to gather his thoughts. He took a long swig of his beer as I watched his sharp Adam's apple rise and fall. I glanced up to see him looking down through his long sandy lashes, and he caught me staring this time.

He set the bottle carefully on a tile. "Ian, I thought you might want to know that no one wants to claim the body. Thomas's body." As if there might be a different body we could be talking about.

"No. That's not right. He has parents in Utah, or no, Idaho, I think. Can they not afford it?"

"They don't want him. Apparently, they dumped him when he came out in high school. He went to stay with an elderly aunt, but after she died, he was mostly living on the streets. The last year of high school his art teacher helped him get the scholarship to RISD. You didn't know that?" he asked as though I really hadn't known Thomas at all. I shook my head dumbly. "I don't think he has anyone to bury him," he finished.

I stared at Jake, trying to make sense of the discrepancy. Thomas and I had talked openly about being gay, coming out. I was sure he'd told me that his parents had been supportive. My mind whirled, reviewing the past, looking for markers that would have given me a hint at the trouble he'd had. I felt wretched, desperately sorry that I could not go to him now that I knew the truth. Perhaps I could have made some kind of difference, so he didn't end up dead. Had I tried to know Thomas a little better, had he told me the truth, would there have been a different outcome? I had no idea of what else the police knew. Only that cryptic, near accusation, and the suggestion that he'd been assaulted by someone.

"Tell me what I need to do. I'll bury him." I took a deep breath, willing the tears down for the hundredth time today, or so it seemed. But really my emotions had been crackly for weeks. Maybe they'd been like that since the morning Jake almost hit me, and I had thought of him again. Maybe it was more like since the leg happened. And maybe I had been working particularly hard at numbing lately.

He nodded. "I'll call you, let you know who to talk to." I guess that's why he came. I thought that it was a nice thing to do for this kid he never knew and who now had no one.

There was a long, empty and awkward pause. I said finally, "Hey! You almost ran me over a month ago. That was you, wasn't it?" I looked at him through narrowed, teasing eyes.

He smiled his crooked smile and nodded. "You scared me half to death stepping out in the street like that. I could have killed you." The irony of the statement was not lost on us as we shared a gaze. "So, you're at RISD now, huh? Drawing teacher?" We were pretending to lighten things up, I supposed.

"Yes, I am. I decided I wanted to concentrate on my painting. Being an adjunct gives me time. RISD was more flexible than RIC." There was a chapter I left out of the story, though, how my long recovery interrupted my tenure track, how my poetry had abandoned me, but... "And you're a detective now, in Providence. That's fine, Jake. Really, I'm happy for you. You made it." I wondered, then, had I known he was so near would it have changed how I'd lived these last few years. "It would have been nice if...if we'd met again before, well, this."

"Huh. Yeah, I guess. But then, there's Arty, so I never..." He shrugged.

"Ah, yes, well. Arty. Arty is no longer in my life—like that anyway. We split a few years ago. Very amicable." I flipped a casual wrist. "We talk often. You know gay men, once in the picture, always in the picture."

"Not always," said Jake quietly.

"No. Not always." The exchange went sideways, then. The conversation stopped. We stared at each other. I'd forgotten how blue his eyes were. I'd tried to recreate that blue in pigment once but could never get it right. A hint of a Veronese green perhaps?

"Why didn't you call me?" There was a note of sad reproach in the question. One for which I had no coherent reply. I frowned a little and shrugged slightly. What could I say? *Well, you see, I've got this mega-canyon where muscle used to be, and I just couldn't bear seeing you scream in terror at it, at me.* Because that was it, wasn't it? I couldn't separate me and my worth from my damaged limb. When both my mother and my lover couldn't, I had stopped trying.

"What happened to your leg, Ian?" And there it was. Jake had never been one for niceties, for small talk, for leading up to things politely. He'd always been right there with the question that needed to be asked, answered. I thought that quality probably made him a formidable foe. I supposed that's what we were now.

I've developed, over the last few years, a nondescript response when talking about my injury that doesn't trigger memories. It involves *not* telling inquirers that the infection had nearly killed me outright at the beginning, and a few times during the hospitalization, that the battle was traumatic and ugly, that it had stripped away more than muscle. "An injury a few years ago, a little muscle involvement. Keeps me gimpy." I tried to keep the tone neutral.

His eyes squinted a little. "Gimpy," he said flatly. My heart plummeted, knowing he could see through the foggy deceit. I never wanted to disappoint him, yet that's all I seemed to do to Jake. But I was not going there. Nope. I smiled back.

Jake's eyes flashed in irritation as he stood, drinking the rest of his beer in a few big gulps. He set the bottle back on the coaster and looked around. "This is a nice place. Come into some money or something?"

Okay. That felt wrong. Who was he now? Detective Quinn, or ex-lover Jake? "Yes. I did."

He raised a suspicious eyebrow and said, "Oh, good. Cool. Nice for you."

I nodded blandly. "I didn't kill him, Jake. You should know that." I meant both that he should know from knowing me and know because I was informing him. I wondered if the distinctions were clear to him as I tried to keep my tone as even and unemotional as I could. Lord, how many elephants were in this room anyway?

"Ian, you gotta understand; I have to let the investigation go where it goes. I, Jake—" He tapped his chest. "—don't *think* you did, but Detective Quinn, doesn't *know*. I could have spoken up, said I knew you, when I saw your name come up in the investigation, but I didn't. Partly because, while the Providence Police Department is pretty forward-thinking, I work really hard at not bringing my sexuality into the picture, *any* picture at work, and I felt if I did now, it would set a, I don't know, a precedent, so I didn't. Also, I'm a new detective, and this case is an opportunity for me. That sounds bad; yeah, I know, but it is. And now Henry and I are pretty deep in it, and I don't want to back out. It feels too late to back out. And I don't want to," he repeated. He sounded angry but with a frantic edge to it, like he was trying to convince himself more than me.

"Yes, yes. I totally understand. I do." I didn't. I was hoping he'd say: "I *know*, of course, I know you didn't do it," so I could pull him into my arms. Shit. I'd loved him back then, and I hadn't known it. Now it was too late. *Christ, Start, you are an idiot.*

Jake left. I looked down at my disheveled state and headed for the shower. My scotch and I would then try some of that Veronese.

*

In the early hours of the morning, lying in bed not sleeping, my cat at my side, a Yeats, learned long ago, came to me:

> *"'Put off that mask of burning gold*
> *With emerald eyes."*
> *"O no, my dear, you make so bold*

To find if hearts be wild and wise,
And yet not cold."

"I would but find what's there to find,
Love or deceit."
"It was the mask engaged your mind,
And after set your heart to beat,
Not what's behind."

"But lest you are my enemy,
I must enquire."
"O no, my dear, let all that be;
What matter, so there is but fire
In you, in me?"

Chapter Four

I managed about five hours of dreamless sleep and woke to another bracing sunny day. Determined not to spend another minute in any state of undress, I showered and put on well-worn jeans and a navy cotton sweater. I actually went so far as to put on socks and loafers today. Downstairs, I fed Clio and made a cup of coffee. Sitting in the kitchen, looking out on my wintery garden, I thought of Thomas. Did we all miss something about him? I had certainly talked to other instructors about him because he was so good. He excelled in illustrative arts, and Hanna and I had talked about him often. Hanna was an illustration professor. She was his biggest fan. But I could not remember anyone expressing concerns about him, or his well-being. The question about his getting beaten niggled at me. I never saw him bruised. At least not during semesters. Who knew about the summers and long breaks?

The finches were attacking the echinacea seeds *en masse*, and for a few moments, I was enraptured by their industriousness. I needed to do something. I could not just sit here waiting, and not even knowing what I was waiting for. I was getting a little sick of myself and my passivity anyway. I thought maybe I'd walk down to the office and talk to Jennifer. See if the police had been up to anything there. Perhaps I'd call a few professors who'd had him in their class. It was something to do anyway.

I'd just put on my charcoal wool overcoat and wrapped a scarf around my neck when my cell phone rang. I'd intended to let it go to voice mail but checked the ID first. Jake.

"Hey, Jake." Smooth. *Oui?*

"Hi, Ian. Look. I was thinking about last night and that Thomas's body is not being claimed. I know I was going to give you information on how to do that, but I decided that it's not such a good idea." I instantly didn't care for his tone. It was a little imperious. Not the Jake I knew or thought I knew.

"Why not? I can't just let him sit in a morgue or go to a pauper's field or some such thing."

There was a little chuckle on the other end. "'Pauper's field' is a little dramatic, Ian. This ain't a Dickens novel." Yes, sarcasm is a great way to influence people. "The state can bury him. It's not fancy, but it's an option. It's just that you doing this will send a wrong message right now. I really don't want you to complicate things even more. And I'm sorry I came to you with that. That was so out of line. I just felt bad for the kid is all."

"'Complicate things even more.' I wish to hell I knew what that meant," I said, irritated by the reminder that I was involved in this case in such an unfair way. Long, long pause. "And who would I be sending a message to? The police? You?"

"No. That's not what I meant." I heard an impatient sigh. "Ian, I want to tell you more. But this is my job. I can't fuck this up. I can't compromise this investigation because of our past. You'll know more when we're further along, okay?"

"So meanwhile, Thomas gets shuffled, I get suspected of...something, murder, really, although no one actually says so, and we are off the table." *Fuck me. Why did I say that? How stupid.*

"I didn't know we were on the table." Jake sounded half amused, which infuriated me.

"Why did you come over last night, Jake?" I was getting pissed off by this entire conversation. Christ, I'd just spent the night trying to recreate the color of his fucking eyes, the little ingrate! Before he could answer, I snarled, "I tell you what, you just go be the best *junior* detective you can be. If something's besmirching my name, *I'll* clear it up. You just find out who killed him." I clicked off. Besmirching. Who says shit like that? I grabbed my cane, slammed and locked the front door, and headed down the street.

From my place on Benefit Street, RISD is only about five blocks. I almost always walk unless I have a load to carry or it's icy. Today, the fresh air, the sun, the bite of the cold was calming and rejuvenating. Despite Jake's call, I was in a better mood. I had a mission. I hadn't fully formed what that mission was, but I was determined to find out what the police thought they had regarding me, and I wanted to find out more about Thomas. It bothered me that I might not have known the real him. I had a suspicion that he'd tried to tell me something, but that perhaps I'd been so typically self-absorbed that I'd missed it. Maybe Jen had heard some conversations Thomas had with other instructors or students. Thomas hung around the office a lot. He was a likable kid, had an easy laugh, I think he was lonely. Come to think of it, I never did see him hanging out with anyone.

As I walked, my phone vibrated. It was Jake. I sighed and let it go to voice mail. What was the use? Jake was off-limits, perhaps even a danger to me. And I had no intention of causing trouble for him. He thought I was guilty anyway. So what was left? Memories and fantasy. I could do that. For the rest of the walk, I remembered some very nice times.

Jen was on her cell phone, texting. She held up a stubby long-nailed finger, pierced. I mean her fingernail was pierced. Well, I supposed it could be worse. I half leaned, half sat against her desk, my back to her, stretching my legs in front of me. Waited. I saw that there were a few portfolios left in the corner where we'd stacked them. I went to check for Thomas's. It wasn't there.

"Hey, Ian. You heard about Thomas, I guess," Jen said.

"I did. Did the cops come here? They came to see me."

"Uh-huh. I figured they would go see you. Actually, they asked a lot of questions about you and Thomas. What's up with that?"

"What did they ask? They're not telling me much."

"So, they were asking about how you and Thomas interacted, whether it was unusual for you to interact with your students as much as you did Thomas. Stuff like that. They asked about the portfolios. If they just sat here unattended. Phht, like they contain secret government plans or something. If I saw anyone messing with them. They wanted to know if our office computers were Mac or PC. They seemed to think that was important. They asked what I knew about Thomas, his friends." She leaned back in her office chair, which tilted way back under her ample form and put her hands behind her head, looking to me to fill in the juicy missing bits.

"They seem to think I was... Jen, does anyone around here, even the faculty, think I had something with Thomas? I mean outside of a teacher/student relationship?"

Jen gave a little snort and said, "You? No way. Too proper. Everyone knows the only teacher shtupping students around here is Pearson."

"Shtupping?" I snorted.

"I read."

I slouched down in one of the cheap black vinyl chairs, the offensive material making unnatural sounds as I slid. I set my elbow on the cold metal armrest, jaw in my hand, thinking. "*Did* Thomas have any friends that you noticed? I never thought about it before, but I'm realizing I never saw him with anyone. He didn't seem to interact much with other classmates."

Jenifer's eyes crossed as she examined her blood-red impaled nail, worrying the little hoop that went through it. A look of hesitancy appeared as she met my eyes.

"You know I hang with Justin, right?" Justin was a flamboyant, fem young man who was out and acting out, outrageous, and charming. From Jen's wary tone, I wasn't sure I was ready for where this conversation was going.

"Yes?"

"So he says, and this is just what he overheard, right? He says that he heard Thomas was on the blade."

I blinked, and blinked, probably blinked again.

"On the blade?" I really hated sounding old, white, and so, so unhip. Wait. I supposed using 'unhip' was unhip. I shook my head to stop that tumble. "What does that even mean, Jen?"

"Prostituting, Ian."

The blinking just would not stop. I did not see that coming. I got a little heated, feeling defensive for Thomas, whom I'd imagined as more naïve, maybe even a little bit of a rube. "Who told Justin that? Do you know? Did you tell the police that?" I was already feeling guilty for not knowing him better. Now this blow. Worse, we'd had plenty of conversations. I should have been more sensitive, listened more, something more than what I had been. In remembering our chats, I realized that I mostly talked about myself and my experiences. Fredrick was right. Some queers are such shits.

"I didn't tell the police anything, Ian. I just mostly said, 'I don't know.' 'Cause I don't, do I? I don't know shit." Now she was getting mad.

"No, of course not. Sorry. That just really surprises me. And I don't think it's true anyway." I paused a moment, thinking about a way to move forward. "Would you do me a huge favor?" I raised a brow and attempted a sweet innocent smile, which probably came off more like a grimace. "Would you ask Justin who said that he was prostituting? And Jen—" I nodded toward her computer. "—look up Thomas's address for me, would you?"

"Okay. You're not going to do something stupid; are you?" Like people know me.

I was off to do something stupid. Thomas didn't live in the dorms. I knew that. But he had hinted at roommates. I thought I'd go by to see if they could shed any light on what happened, not just to Thomas, but what connected me to his murder, and as a result what Jake might believe. Did he really think I would have sex with a vulnerable young student?

Thomas's address was on Waterman Street, the other side of Brown, just south of Wayland. It was a long walk for me, but it was only late morning, and I could take breaks at the myriad of coffee shops that invariably dot college neighborhoods. I decided to walk through the Brown campus. Being outside felt lovely. The campus's lawns were a dull dormant green and the flower beds empty. Sculptures seemed to mimic the bare trees, arms reaching, trunks twisting. Students suffered in the cold to smoke cigarettes. But even in winter, it's a handsome campus with an eclectic mixture of Victorian, Romanesque Revival, Italianate, modern, and contemporary architecture. The quads are a great place to take students to draw when finer weather beckons.

I stopped at an independent cafe on Thayer Street for a pastry and an espresso. I checked my phone and saw that Jake had left a message: "Ian, I don't know what you meant about clearing your name, but I'm telling you in no uncertain terms: do not get involved in this investigation. Call me." His tone was harsh, cold. I did not need this bullshit. I deleted it and concentrated on my eclair. As I licked a blob of creme filling from my upper lip, I contemplated eating real food one of these days. Or not.

"Call me." Jake was sending so many mixed messages I couldn't seem to land anywhere. I supposed I was guilty of it too. It was just that I understood mine—fear, pure fear. Fear of my desire to trust Jake. Fear of my level of attraction to him. Fear that I didn't know him as well as I thought I did, and fear that he didn't know me at all. And the familiar fear that the reaction to the "new deteriorated" me was going to be a universal reaction, and fear that I would never find out. My hand unconsciously wandered to my outer thigh, my fingertips delving into that deep scar. But the overriding fear was that he thought me guilty.

By the time I got to the address Jen had written down on a jaunty pink Post-it, the day had warmed a little under the white winter sun, and I took my overcoat off. The building was a meticulously maintained converted white clapboard house, a giant box really, but not new architecture. It had probably been a tenement at one time, housing Providence's working-class families. There were two barren trees on each side of the walkway, but no lawn—just scrupulously raked dirt. The building had three stories containing ten or so apartments, depending on how it was carved up. There was a bank of mailboxes at the bottom of the entry steps. More than ten units, more like fifteen. A few studios then. They were numbered simply 1, 2, 3... No hint as to level, with last names punched out with those old fashioned DYMO plastic labels. Wilson was 12. Top floor probably.

The front door led to an entry foyer where there were two lines of buzzers. I pressed 12 Wilson. Nothing. What did I think was going to happen by coming here? It seemed a little silly now as I waited. Maybe I should just press a bunch of buttons to see if some fool would open the door. It worked in the movies. But I'm a skinny, crippled chump. In other words: no balls.

I turned to head back home just as someone was coming in. I pretended to ponder the Post-it with Thomas's address as he unlocked the door. I nodded at him and said, "Hey I'm looking for Thomas Wilson. Do you know what apartment he's in?"

He looked at me for a long moment. Deciding I was no danger, I guess, but not trusting either, he offered, hesitantly, "Um, Thomas doesn't live here anymore."

"I know he was... He's dead." I decided it couldn't hurt just to be upfront with this guy. He looked to be in his forties, a medium build, scant curly hair on top, but a veritable hedge around the sides, a little beer gut, a pleasant face. "Look, I was an instructor of his at RISD. I'm just trying to figure out what happened to him, why. Did you know him?"

"The police already talked to everyone. I told 'em what I knew." He was in work clothes, those thick canvas pants the color of dun and an orange safety vest. He was carrying a hardhat.

"What did you tell them?" I tried to sound casual, conversational.

"Oh, you know, I told 'em he was a nice kid. He kept crazy hours. Gave some of us Christmas cards that he drew. I didn't know him that well. Not to talk to anyway. Just to say hi."

I wanted to ask if the officers asked about me, or a professor but thought better of it. "Do you know if he had any roommates?"

"No. I don't think so. I'm on the second floor, and he's on the third—was. He had an efficiency in the back corner over mine. They're kinda small for more than one person. But the students can pile 'em in. Rents are high here." He had a Rhode Island accent, longish *a*'s. Different from a Boston accent, not so pinched and nasal. I liked it.

"Did he have people over, have parties?" I didn't know what I was trawling for. I think I wanted to learn that he wasn't always alone, that he had friends, or maybe that he didn't have a string of men walking in and out on a nightly basis.

"Couldn't tell ya. Can't (cahn't) remember any parties." He moved to go in. Hmm, right under the kid and he didn't know if Thomas had people over. When I'd been renting my apartment in East Providence, I could hear every footstep of my upstairs neighbors. I knew when they were entertaining, knew when they were watching TV; hell, I knew when they were having sex. Maybe I was overanalyzing. Perhaps I wanted to solve the puzzle. The guy seemed straightforward enough. I was struggling with how straightforward I was with myself. I needed a better plan than wandering around the city, guessing at what I wanted to know, what I needed to know, and why.

I wondered about all of his drawings and illustrations. What would become of them? It was probably all that was left of him, but according to Jake, there was no one around to honor that. God, would that be me one day? A wave of panic caught me short of breath, with a racing heart. Leaning against the outer doorjamb, I calmed my breathing and asked, "Is there a manager here? I'm wondering if anyone's come to clean his apartment out, like family or anything."

"No manager here. You have to call that number on the sign." He pointed to a paper on the door window that stated Addams Property Management and a phone number. I entered it in my phone. He started to go into the building when he stopped and turned back to me. "I just remembered, sometime last year there was a big commotion up there. Like a fight or something. Someone musta called the cops 'cause they came. But I don't know what it was about, and there's been no trouble since." He shrugged and shut the inner door on me.

I headed down the steps. Well, that was a little something, right? My walk wasn't a complete blowout. It gave me a millimeter of confidence. As a result, I immediately phoned Jake and left a terse message telling him that I didn't give a fuck what message it sent to whom. I wanted the information on getting Thomas buried.

Chapter Five

After seven days, during which the Medical Examiner's Office could not find any relatives to claim his body, Thomas was released to me. I arranged for Pereira's Funeral Home to get him. I chose a simple pine casket, against the salesman's advice touting other models as being "impervious to outside elements." Rita and I planned an informal graveside service for after the actual burial. I chose North Burial Ground which is near my home and RISD. It is beautifully historic, with ancient trees, the arms of which seem to shelter loved ones bearing names like Patience, Constance, Resolve, and one for "Our Little Frankie" who had a lamb atop his stone. I liked to think maybe Thomas had gone there to draw the old elaborate statuary that adorns the ancient graves. It was a place rich with light and shadow, figure, and architecture, and I'd often encouraged students to go there to draw. I wondered if I still would.

Rita and I were the only ones there when they lowered the casket. Afterward, Fredrick came to the site, as did a few professors, including Hanna and Jen. Detective Ransom and Jake were there. "Looking for their murderer," Jen said snidely. She'd also said that Justin was going to come, and he'd talk to me about what he'd heard, but he never did show up. It had been raining all morning, and although it stopped, the wind was up, blowing our hair into impossible dos. We'd dressed for the ceremony. Rita in a knit heather-brown woolen pencil skirt and a brown double-breasted coat; Jen was a little less formal in black leggings and a long sweater that hung below her puffy parka. I'd chosen my Canali charcoal flannel suit with a subtle coral stripe and a white shirt and a gray and coral paisley tie. The suit was my favorite. I thought Thomas would have appreciated it. He liked fashion. Jake's suit was a blue that was not quite navy, with a sheen that reflected his eyes, which he carefully kept directed away from mine. It was only three, but in winter it would be dark by four, and the sun was belatedly trying to burn through the clouds. We each spoke a few words of remembrance about Thomas. I planned to read a poem. The wind whipped at the pages of the book as if telling me to stop, to give this farce up. Clichéd, perhaps, at funerals, I nevertheless chose to read Housman's *Goodnight*.

> *Goodnight; ensured release,*
> *Imperishable peace,*
> *Have these for yours,*
> *While sea abides, and land,*
> *And earth's foundations stand,*
> *and heaven endures.*

> *When earth's foundations flee,*
> *nor sky nor land nor sea*
> *At all is found*
> *Content you, let them burn:*
> *It is not your concern;*
> *Sleep on, sleep sound.*

The faculty stayed a few minutes to chat about Thomas, the upcoming year, complaints about the administration. It was better to end on a less dismal note, a striving for normalcy. We discussed the party that the department dean gave every year before the start of the second semester. This year the invitation said that dress was "optional," and for a few moments, we joked about the benefits of nudity. We drifted off, each heading back to our established lives.

I stopped to ask Hanna if she had any insight into Thomas's life. She told me that they really didn't talk much except about art and future plans. "He wanted to go to New York. To make a name there in illustration. He was realistic about the competition, but he said he'd never forgive himself if he didn't try." That sounded like him. Forever optimistic.

"Do you remember him ever coming in bruised up or anything?" I asked.

"Yeah, the police asked the same thing. I don't remember anything like that. But, like I told them, I didn't have him in class every semester, and I try not to teach summers. Ian, they asked a lot of questions about you. Kind of ishy questions..." Hanna left off obviously hoping for some details from me.

"I know. Don't worry about it, Hanna. They're on a wrong track there." Did that diversion make it worse? It seemed like making a statement about my innocence in all of it; murder, inappropriate behavior, would sound premature and a little strident.

As we walked away, Ransom came up alongside me. Jake headed toward the few parked cars. "Nice simple service, Professor Start; that's what I would want, I think." He pulled a half-smoked cigar from his front pocket and slowed to light it. I waited. "I wonder if we could stop by for a few minutes." He spoke around his stogie, distorting the aspirates.

"Now, you mean?" I'd wanted to, planned on, going home and drinking slowly and steadily the rest of the night with a red sable paintbrush in my hand. At Ransom's nod, I capitulated. "Yes, sure. I'll meet you there."

Ransom and Jake were at my house before Rita and I arrived. By then the sun had fully set. They'd parked illegally on the street and stood looking up at my front door. I pulled into my drive which angles up a small hill to the level of my patio and back door. Rita and I walked down the slope and wondered what they were looking at so intently.

"Start, any chance you left your front door standing wide open?" Ransom asked.

Hell and damn was my thought as I stared up into my foyer, the door, indeed, standing wide open. "Nope. Not a chance. I don't think so anyway. No." I looked at Rita for some support. We'd gone out the back door today. When had I used the front door last? She shrugged. She has a second entrance on the other side of the Brownstone that she uses to get to my back door; there are concrete steps that go up to my level. She wouldn't have seen my door. I didn't remember looking up as we left.

"Stay here," ordered Ransom. They headed up the stairs, pulling their service revolvers from the holsters under their arms. They both held them at their sides and pointing down as they entered. Rita and I stared at each other. I had expensive stuff in there, sure, but it was my own artwork and writing that I most cared about, and the art that I'd gathered from friends, students, colleagues.

And Clio! Where was my cat? I really did start to panic at that point. I knew she'd go out. She was a bolter. She'd usually bolt into the back garden and then stop immediately, disoriented, giving me time to scoop her up with a head rubbing and a kiss.

I immediately started a frantic call: "Clio, here kitty, kitty, *pssst, pssst, pssst*" over and over. Rita joined me. I wandered back up the drive to the yard and called some more. Nothing. In the dark, my garden was full of inky stick figures bouncing menacingly in the gloom. *Shit.* What if someone did go in and did something to her? I did an awkward modified half skip back to the front. Rita had been going up and down the street, calling. She shook her head.

I climbed the steps and entered just as Ransom was coming down the stairs from the second floor. Meeting in the dining area, he said, "I think someone went through your papers in your den. You want to take a look around, see if anything's missing? I'm going to call it in." He was having trouble catching his breath. *Smokers,* I thought ungenerously. But who was I to talk? He lacked lung muscle; I lacked leg. I headed for the stairs.

"I don't suppose you saw my cat, did you?" I could hear Rita outside calling, calling. She wouldn't quit until I asked her to. I wasn't going to ask her to. *Yer a selfish prick, Start.*

"Did not. It got out, huh?" Ransom's dismissive tone rankled, but I continued up the stairs, calling her name now and then. The uppermost flight of stairs empties onto a little landing with an overstuffed loveseat and club chair in gray cotton duck. They'd both seen better days, now marbled with gobs and smears of oil paints. I often sat there to take a break from painting. Sometimes I'd find that I'd fallen asleep on the small sofa, bad leg curled up to fit, my good leg flung over bad, touching the floor.

I checked the studio quickly and saw nothing unusual. In my den, however, papers had been spilled to the floor and spread over my desk, a massive oak partners affair that I'd had hauled up from the outside and maneuvered through the windows. Jake was standing at one of the windows on the other side of my desk. The partner side.

"My laptop's gone." I stopped to think of what I'd actually lost, which I realized was very little as I am obsessive about backups, using the cloud and thumb drives consistently. I checked the top drawer where I kept the flash drives. They were gone too. But still, everything important got automatically uploaded. "My flash drives are gone too." This burglary didn't make sense. I had more valuable things. "Why just my laptop and drives?" I wasn't addressing anyone in particular, but Jake answered with a shrug.

"Could be for passwords, bank information, credit card numbers..." Ransom said from behind me. Rita was coming up the stairs and clomping footsteps announced the arrival of the patrol unit. "We can talk more after you make your report."

I sat at my desk, while the others sat or stood around as the uniformed men asked me the basic questions: Did I lock my doors? Had I seen anyone suspicious in the neighborhood? All I could manage was to utter defeated yeses and noes. The patrolmen said the lock had probably been picked, not too hard to do, and relatively quick, and asked if anyone else had a key?

"Erm, Ian?" Rita interrupted, "I forgot all about it until now, but remember about a month ago I lost my keys? Your key was on the ring too. Did you change your locks?" I shook my head. "Well do you think they used that one?" She directed that question to one of the patrol officers. "It was just my keys, so I don't see how they'd know where I live."

"It's doubtful, but you never know. You should change your locks, Mr. Start." The officers wrapped it up and left. Rita took them down and said she'd call for Clio again and then lock up.

"Professor Start," Ransom began, "I'm gonna let you in on what we found at Thomas's apartment. First of all, he was shot while sitting at his computer. It looked as though he'd been typing an email addressed to the dean of your department. The contents stated that you had been pressuring him for a, well, a physical relationship and that you had, as he put it, or should I say, as he typed it, 'groped him.'" Ransom stopped and seemed to wait for my response. Jake was still looking out the window, his jaw working, grinding away at some invisible grievance.

I was gobsmacked, as my father would say. The detectives had hinted at evidence of an intimate relationship, but to have it come from Thomas was preposterous. I'd never, ever come close to being inappropriate with any student. We'd talked about being gay, experiences dating, negotiating relationships and so forth, but nothing sexual, overt or implied. I sat back in my desk chair, speechless, my mouth hanging open. "No." Was my ineffectual response. My knuckles began to tingle. I knew the itch would start soon, but I was resolute in my conviction to refrain from scratching.

Ransom went on, "And, we found a typed letter that looks like it's from you, that seems to support his email. The letter was in his portfolio along with your grade sheet with the comments on it. The letter was sexually explicit, requesting sexual favors." He sat back in the chair and crossed his legs as if he had all the time in the world to listen to me deny it.

And deny I did. "Detective Ransom"—I leaned forward in my chair—"I have no idea what's going on here, but none of those things happened, and to tell you the truth, I do not believe that Thomas wrote that email, and I certainly did not write that letter." My intestines stirred unpleasantly. I started to sweat, and my heart felt like it wanted to invent a new kind of rhythm. I was clearly heading into a full-blown panic attack. One thing I learned while coping with the infection was how to handle anxiety attacks. I knew that if there was no stopping it, the best thing to do was to admit to it, ride it out and breathe deeply. I was able to put up one hand and gasp "panic attack" to Ransom before I folded my arms on my desk to pillow my forehead. I stared at the floor and concentrated on my breath. I heard someone walk away, then return after a moment or two. This was a bad one, unrelenting, pounding heart; surely this one would kill me. No—those were the thoughts I was supposed to battle. Mastering my self-talk more effectively and deep breathing helped calm my heart, but the shaking and sweating continued. Finally, I lifted my head. There was a bottle of water in front of me. Jake.

"Sorry, thanks," I muttered. The water helped ease the sweating. I continued to shake, and now, to my embarrassment, I could feel tears welling up. I felt weak. I knew I appeared overly emotional and totally unmanly. Christ. I wiped my hands over my face and looked at Ransom. "So, now what?" My thought was that I'd most likely be arrested.

Ransom shook his head as if I'd spoken the thought aloud. "Well, I would have liked to have our tech team look at your laptop to rule you in or out as a suspect, but that won't happen now, obviously." He paused and looked at Jake, who shrugged his shoulders, again, still staring out the window.

Jake sighed loudly and looked toward me but not exactly at me. "It is kind of odd that the laptop gets stolen now, don't you think?" he said with an undeniably sarcastic lilt. Before a rejoinder was even possible, he added, "We'd like to take your cell phone back to the station for a few days, if you agree to it. We'd have to get a warrant otherwise. Ian, right now, it looks as though there are really only two scenarios: either you killed Thomas Wilson, or you are being set up." He said this straight-faced, emotionless, as though I were a stranger.

For a moment I felt stunted, like a child thrown into a room full of adults and having to instantly figure out how to behave in order to avoid getting into trouble. I was not outraged, although I felt I ought to be. I understood his conclusions intellectually. But I did not feel passive emotionally. I wanted to be heard and believed when I said I didn't do it. I was overwhelmingly frustrated that my words could not be evidence because they were all I had in my defense. It pissed me off that I did care whether Ransom believed me on a personal level regardless of what sounded like pretty damning evidence. And Jake. I knew he couldn't really look at me because he believed I did it.

Without a word I pulled my phone out of my suit jacket and handed it over.

*

After they left, I changed into jeans and a sweatshirt, shoved my feet into fleecy slippers and headed down to call for my cat again, needing the only thing that was constant in my life. I stood at the back door staring into the yard, calling... Nothing. When I turned back to the kitchen, she was sitting at the opening into the dining area looking at me like I'd lost my mind. I'd already felt close to insanity, and she wasn't helping any. "Unbelievable" was all I could say to her. I called Rita to let her know that the damnable feline had been in the house the whole time. She laughed and asked if I'd eaten anything. When I admitted I had not, she demanded that I come down and share a frittata and salad with her. I grabbed a glass, poured my scotch and headed down the side steps.

It was getting colder and the clouds had moved back in. A silver glow from the reflection of Providence's lights lit the way down. Rita's door stood ajar, so I went in. When I'd remodeled the apartment, I'd left it an open floor plan. Natural light was limited to the front and the anterior side windows. The back of the unit butted up against earth so leaving the space open helped disperse the light. Rita had furnished it with Danish modern angles and simplicity in pale neutrals with surprise pops of red and purple. Light and delicate contrasted to my large overstuffed leathers and tweedy wools. It fit her petite frame and her feathery, graceful way of moving through the world.

As we ate her simple mushroom and cheese frittata, I filled her in on what Ransom and Jake had said. She chewed and shook her head, looking at her plate in concentration. "Maybe you should call a lawyer, Ian," she said, meeting my eyes with her dark chocolate orbs.

"I don't need a lawyer, Rita. I'll call one if I get arrested." She flattened her lips in frustration. I smiled sweetly. I set down my fork and stared at the empty plate. "I feel broken." Tears started to well. Again. "I'm crying at everything—every frustration, every hope, the slightest disappointment."

"Every hope, huh? That's a new addition to your vocabulary." It was a gentle tease. I'd regaled her with my catalog of negative assertions and attitudes for as long as we'd been friends. I was aware I'd probably pushed "Ian burnout" with her, but her even demeanor, her peaceful countenance led me like a thirsty beast to her unending trough of comfort. "What's the hope?" she asked.

I didn't want to say it was Jake, but it was. I was embarrassed that I couldn't help wanting him, and I couldn't temper the desire, or wouldn't, and by the reality that my hope was untenable, that this was a man who now saw me as... Seeing him again seemed to solder long broken connections in my brain, the part that connected to my heart. I wanted to be able to feel vulnerable again. As it was, I felt like I'd go just to the end of a leash before getting yanked back into defensiveness and an emotional deadness.

"I think the hope is that I don't want to be lonely. That makes no sense." I poured more wine. *I hope to get drunk.* Rita stood and walked over to her long, lean couch, I followed her, bringing the bottle, settling next to her for warmth.

"I think the hope is that you admit you're lonely." She rested her head on my shoulder. I could smell her spicy shampoo and feel her crunchy curls on my cheek.

"I feel like I only want to give up my loneliness for Jake. But that leaves me nowhere, right? He's a cop who thinks I murdered someone." Suddenly, it all seemed so ridiculous, and I started to laugh, a desperate laugh. I was seeing the whole situation as Theater of the Absurd. Rita sat back and looked at me. I was laughing so hard tears were coming. "So absurd" was all I could say. And then, abruptly, I was crying big, gasping, gulping sobs. "I'm fucking insane."

"How do you know?" asked Rita, handing me a paper napkin and rubbing my back.

"That I'm insane?"

"No, you idiot, know that Jake thinks you murdered Thomas. Did you ask him?" She was looking at me evenly.

"Tsuh, of course not. I don't think that would be appropriate, do you?" I had somewhat reined in my crying jag and lay my head on the back of her couch, staring at the rings of light the lamps cast on the ceiling and at the adjacent double shadows.

"You should call him, Ian. Figure out what you are going to do with these feelings. Know if there's a way forward or a possibility of one or not. Know what he's thinking, at least."

"No... I think not. I'm more comfortable not knowing." But that wasn't true, and I knew it. What I was comfortable with was not asking. Not knowing was killing me.

"Call. Him." I shook my head. I picked up her TV remote and found an old film noir that fit my bleak mood, *Laura*. I pulled Rita's oversized fuzzy throw over both of us and poured more wine. I felt a little better for the cry, I guessed, but I wished I could go back a month to where I felt more stable. Or, better yet, go back a few years, before the real damage had happened.

I woke to a dark apartment. I was still on Rita's couch, but only barely. She'd covered me with the throw. I was lying on my side, head on a velvet cushion. I could hear her soft snore on the other side of her wooden screen. I rose and headed out the side door, shutting and locking it quietly. It was snowing lightly, tiny little flakes that fluttered around the streetlamp like gnats.

Chapter Six

It was still snowing in the morning. The trifling flakes from last night had morphed into big fat ones that were beginning to collect on the dead garden foliage. I wanted to called Jen to ask about Justin, whether he was still willing to talk to me about Thomas, but without my cell phone, that would have to wait. I only gave my landline number out to a few people and very rarely used it, and all my contact numbers were on my cell anyway. With time on my hands and a storm settling in, I ate cold cereal with my coffee and headed up to my studio. I'd started a new painting. A dog I'd seen in an empty lot. A dog that looked as senseless as I was feeling these days. Greens and browns with line and texture, a junkyard dog that had lost its ability to frighten. Flesh suffering purchase in age hanging on its body like chains. I worked long into the night, stopping to step back occasionally, and only once to eat an energy bar I had stashed in a kitchenette drawer. Around seven I poured a scotch and fell back into the rhythm.

Sometimes these days, when I paint, I lose a conscious sense of self. I'm not aware of seeing what I'm painting, and I get lost in the rhythm of the back and forth of laying paint on canvas. I have sometimes come back to awareness in awe of what I painted: the composition not being the vision I'd started with. Rita thought it a kind of dissociation. Good work, I thought, but I sometimes felt fraudulent, as though someone else were painting, using my body as a tool. Rita once said these were closer to the inner me than my earlier paintings. We both knew that by earlier she meant before the infection, back when I could write.

In the early morning, I slept for a few hours on the loveseat and then started again. I repeated this scenario one more time. By midmorning on the second day (or third?), I was exhausted, and that exhaustion landed me back in my own skin and bones. I could see the painting. The dog was no longer harmless looking—it was angry and sick with savagely cold eyes, and its left front leg was raw, bereft of skin with muscle and tendon exposed. I'd only had a vague awareness of what I'd been painting. I sat on my stool and wondered if there was something seriously wrong with me. I dropped my paintbrush in my turps, forgoing a decent cleaning, swallowed the last of my scotch, and headed to my bedroom. I stripped and fell into bed and into an uneasy sleep until early evening when I woke hungry and headachy. I stunk of sweat and oil paint and turpentine. After showering, I put on worn jeans and a white cotton Henley and headed down for soup, something easy. I did not feel rested. I felt a little ill.

The stairs in my brownstone are all contained in the space that is my entryway, which juts out to the side like an addition, so I come down from my second floor facing my front door. On the floor, below the mail slot, there was a little package in a bubble mailer. It was my cell phone. It hadn't gone through the mail. Ransom must have dropped it off. I pulled it out, along with a handwritten note, an unsigned receipt, and an addressed envelope.

> *I knocked and rang but no answer. Maybe you're painting. Could you sign the receipt and send it back? Jake.*

My stomach churned a little, and I couldn't tell, in my current state, whether it was nausea or excitement. I couldn't keep doing this, allowing myself to be yanked up and down by out-of-control emotions. I needed to impose some limits on how I was thinking and feeling about Jake. Laughably, it only occurred to me now that I didn't even know if Jake was available. He was handsome, smart, and kind, would have no trouble attracting someone. Really, it would be surprising if he was unattached. At any rate, the barriers were too high for me, and I needed to stop—stop fantasizing, concentrate on other things. Thomas for instance. I wanted to know what had happened, why. I'd missed something, and it had cost him. I was convinced of that.

With my cell phone back (fully charged!), I called Fredrick to see if he wanted to go for dinner somewhere and then come back here and have a drink. Or better, get takeout and eat here. He said he'd pick up vindaloo at Kebabs and be over. Vindaloo from Kebabs was hot enough to burn the fuck out of our mouths. We loved it. It could take my mind off almost anything.

Waiting for Fredrick, I called Jen to ask if she'd heard from Justin.

"No. And it's weird. It goes straight to voice mail, and I've been calling for a couple of days."

"Maybe he lost his phone or something, Jen."

"Hmm. Maybe, but he usually calls me every day. I haven't heard from him for a couple of days now. But maybe he went to visit someone or something. I'll keep trying."

"Okay. Thanks, Jen. Hey, give me his phone number, and I can try too." She said she'd text it to me, and a few seconds after we disconnected, my phone vibrated.

Winter break made tracking students more difficult I realized. They go home for holidays or travel. This part of the city quiets down a little. The traffic thins. The loud radios are quiet. And when the snow falls, like tonight, the hush is sweet.

The rat-a-tat of Fredrick's knock interrupted the quiet. We set the takeout containers on the kitchen counter, spooned a variety of the meats in thick, fiery sauce onto basmati rice. I poured a lovely Moscato Rosé from Northern Italy, a delicate sweet to counter the burn. We took our plates to the front room. I'd laid a fire earlier, and I chose George Shearing with Michael Feinstein for background music. We settled into eating, sweating and swearing, bitching about academia and politics afterward.

Fredrick asked what I'd been working on. I sent him up to look at the dog. I heard a shout and a guffaw and something that sounded like "It's mooning."

"What?" I shouted back.

He clumped down the stairs and said, "It's de Kooning. De Kooning paints a dog, and it's just as scary as his paintings of women with their toothy grins and scary bosoms." He made a mad grin to demonstrate. We laughed. "I like it though. I don't think you'll sell it, but it'll show well." Fredrick. He liked everything I painted, but what did he know? He was an English teacher.

Fredrick and I met when I was on a tenure track in the creative writing department at the RIC before I got sick. Or injured. Which was it? Sick or injured? There was a difference between the two, but I vacillated on which described me. Fredrick was there for me after Arty left. He kept me from drinking too much, brought a chuckle or two during a time I never thought I'd see the humor in anything again.

He was an attractively beefy man from the West Indies, his accent like song. When he smiles and laughs, he presents a perfect inverted triangle with full cheeks at two points and the endpoint a dimpled chin. He wears a scant beard that extends from his sideburns framing his jaw and chin. A mustache, also scant, rests above his lip. Fredrick loves to laugh, and his laugh is a beautiful thing, deeply resonant; he leans in to make it everyone's. He was forced to leave Trinidad due to his homosexuality. He was not exactly rejected by his family, but they were embarrassed by him. As a young college student, he'd been caught kissing a boy, was kicked out and outed. His grandfather, who had become a persona non grata when he abandoned the family to come to America, agreed to take him in. He helped Fredrick finish college at CUNY and then he got full scholarships to earn a masters at URI and to get his doctorate from Boston College. He currently taught undergraduate literature at RIC.

Fredrick almost always had a new lover. He was steadfastly monogamous, but not interested in long-term partnerships. We'd talk casually about relationships, but we didn't tend to share deeply. We shared similar politics and views of academia passionately though, as we did tonight. Over cognac, warmed by the snapping fire, we talked about writing. About my impotence. I'd not been able to write, not a line, since the injury. *See? Now it's injury.*

"Don't you think it's weird that you can paint but not write?" Fredrick asked.

"I don't know...painting is more... mmm... spontaneous, visceral for me. It doesn't take a conscious language, more of a physical language, if that makes sense. I can switch off, and it happens. Writing, I have to tune in, and that's where I'm stuck. I can't tune in." I looked away, into the fire, with a sigh. I felt lost not writing. Writing grounded me. Made me feel a part of the world, connected to it, partaking in it, tasting it. Painting kept me afloat emotionally but floating, directionless.

"You're grieving your leg," he stated.

My gaze snapped to his. Fredrick did not usually speak so intentionally or express such insight.

"I think I'm afraid to grieve my leg in any but the most abstract of ways," I responded. He nodded. We lapsed into a companionable silence, staring at the fire, sipping our drinks.

"It wouldn't bother *me*, you know." I knew he wasn't making an overture, just wanting to remind me that there were good, accepting people out there. I nodded.

He left shortly after, the snow only a remnant slush at the sides of the street. I headed to bed with Clio at my heel. I slept deeply without dreams.

*

The morning was sunny, cold, but still. Feeling rested, I vowed to keep busy, to not mope. I showered and dressed in my most comfortable jeans and an olive-green merino sweater. Down in the kitchen, I made my coffee, fed the vocally demanding beast, and attacked my cell phone, ordering a new MacBook, checking email, texting Rita to confirm that she'd be my guest at the faculty party this weekend. I brought either Rita or Fredrick every year. Fredrick enjoyed them more, but Rita was prettier.

I also called the number for Thomas's landlord. I explained who I was and that I wanted to know what would become of his belongings, especially his artwork. He answered my questions politely, without curiosity.

Thomas was paid through this month, so the landlord could not rent the apartment legally, even though he knew Thomas was not coming back. Then he'd have to send a certified letter to Thomas (how silly) informing him that he had a set amount of days to claim his belongings, which the landlord would store. After that, belongings could be sold or disposed of. He said that he was also going to send Thomas's parents the letter. He'd gotten their address from the police. I asked if I could have the address, too, which he supplied.

On an impulse, I asked him if there was any chance I could just look at what was there, as far as Thomas's art. He'd hesitated a long moment before agreeing. Since he couldn't get in trouble with the lessee, he supposed it would be okay as long as I didn't take anything. He couldn't meet me until Monday though. We agreed on two in the afternoon. As my last item on my to-do list, I called Jen to see if she'd heard from Justin.

"I haven't," she said, "and now I'm getting worried. Do you think we should call someone?"

"Does admissions have an emergency contact for him?"

"I'll call and find out. Should I call it if they do?"

"On second thought, let's not call anyone until we know more. Where does he live, Jen?"

"He's in the dorms. He had a roommate, but he moved in with his girlfriend. I asked him if he's seen Justin around, and he hasn't. Ian, Justin and I are pretty tight, so he'd tell me if he were leaving town or going home. Something's wrong."

"Does the roommate still have a key to the room?" I also thought this situation was a little odd; Jen asked about what he knows about a murdered boy, and now he's nowhere to be found. "We could go check it out."

"Ooh, good idea. Let me text him. I'll call you right back." We clicked off. I sat, bouncing my good leg nervously, sipping coffee. I had to admit that even though digging around was a little eerie, it was also slightly exhilarating. Jen didn't call, she texted:

HE HAS KEY WILL MEET US THERE IN 30 MIN. OK?

I texted *OK* back and went to put on my chukkas, overcoat, and scarf. Grabbing my cane, I headed down the street to meet Jen at the office. Justin's room was in East Hall, about a block away. We waited outside the dorms for his roommate, Dave, who led us to the second floor and halfway down the front hall. The rooms were laid out around the perimeter of the building, with bathrooms and showers in the middle.

Dave gave a short rap and, without waiting, unlocked the door. We all piled into the small space. The room was the ubiquitous dorm design: a twin bed on each side of a window, cheap desks, plastic chairs, and unimaginative linoleum. It was, essentially, empty. One of two wardrobes stood open and bare. The other, Dave said, had been his. He opened it anyway. Empty. We opened drawers. Nothing. There were a few scraps of paper, old announcements, takeout menus. But everything that would have indicated occupancy was gone, except that the bed was still made: a cheap comforter, a pillow, and sheets.

"What the hell?" said Jen.

"Maybe he moved in with someone?"

Jen shook her head. "I don't think so, Ian. He never ever said anything about moving. He kinda liked the dorm. He got a lot of attention here. We should ask around." Except that, at almost every door we knocked on, there was no answer. Whether they were out for the day or for the winter break, we had no idea. Only two people came to their doors, and they both told us they hadn't seen or heard from Justin since the end of the semester. Dave hung around and knocked on some doors too. Without being asked, he told us he didn't know Justin very well—they rarely talked—but he seemed like a nice guy. He took off after that.

Jen and I stood outside again and looked at each other. "C'mon, Jen. Let's go get some lunch. And a beer." She nodded, looking worried, dejected. We headed over to Harry's. Over their wee burgers, a stout for me, a pale ale for Jen, we speculated on whether Justin's disappearance had anything to do with his knowledge about Thomas.

"Justin is impulsive, Lord knows," Jen offered.

"So you think there's no connection?"

"I just think he would have called me if there was something fabulous going on with him, he'd want to flaunt it. And if there was nothing fabulous going on, then he'd return my calls and texts." She was tapping her elaborate nails on her glass.

"So what? That leaves one, he's impulsive, two, he's predictable, or three, he's offline on purpose. And what does that mean?"

"Fuck all if I know," Jen sighed, her shoulders drooping.

Without saying anything to Jen, I thought there was a fourth option; that Justin *couldn't* respond to Jen. But was that just me being dramatic, or *was* there any substance to our worry? Because of the notes left behind, it seemed what was going on was confined to just two people: Thomas and me. Though, if someone had information about what had happened, they could be in danger, I supposed. It would be nice if I had an expert to talk to about my thoughts and speculations. A flash of Jake, supine in my bed in East Providence, his face flushed and pupils blown as he took me in, his legs pulled back, knees spread... *Stop this. I must stop this!*

After lunch, Jen headed back to the office. I walked home, up old narrow North Court Street, ever careful of icy spots. I felt stymied. I didn't know how to find my way to what I needed to know, or if I could. Maybe whatever happened to Thomas would remain a mystery. More than once, I'd wanted to call Ransom (Jake, really, but I was intent on denying that) to find out what was going on. There had been no more accusations, inferred or otherwise, and I hadn't been arrested. Maybe I was in the clear. But one thing was left: Who would want to direct suspicion toward me? Why? I'm a pretty inoffensive fellow. I've not purloined lovers, insulted wives or husbands, stolen from anyone, and I wield no power. Perhaps I was just convenient. *Who* would find me convenient? Students, faculty? It did seem related to school somehow. That was the only tangible connection to Thomas. So that left only faculty, students, or admin. No, not necessarily. What about the more intangible? School could be a secondary connection. If someone who knew Thomas also knew about his connections at school, knew something about his instructors...like shared sexual orientation perhaps. That felt like a stretch though.

At home, I did long overdue chores grudgingly. I was feeling disconnected and irritable. With nothing particularly absorbing or appealing to do, I thought about Thomas himself. About the crime of being shot in the head, the coldness or anger that it must take to put a weapon to another's cranium and shoot. I tried to avoid imagining gray matter exiting along with the heart and flame contained therein. By early evening, I just wanted a glass of wine and an uncomplicated movie in bed, with a mouthy blue-eyed cat.

Chapter Seven

Rita looked gorgeous in a snug black velvet dress and pale-rose velvet mules with a little heel that she called a "kitten heel." I let her choose my suit; she chose my gray Corneliani sharkskin. I chose a pale-lavender shirt and a silver silk tie with deep-purple squares. When I got the settlement, Fredrick taught me how to dress, but more importantly, shop. Before that, I was strictly Macy's and Men's Warehouse. I was doing an adequate job, but Fredrick knew style. Better yet, he knew fit. He reminded me that fashion was art, and he was right—I'd always enjoyed the art of fashion—I just never saw how it applied to me. When I started putting on these higher-end clothes, at least the few suits that I invested in, I saw the difference—I felt the difference. I started to apply what I knew about color, form, and function to what I covered my body with. I also felt guilty spending money on what I'd previously viewed as frivolous, and a little vain, but Fredrick had said, "Then balance it with something meaningful. It's not like you're any part of the one percent. You just have some disposable income."

The dean's parties were always well catered with abundant food and top-shelf booze. We were greeted by her husband, Allen Kindrick. He was of old Rhode Island money originally earned from the textile trade, now by high-end clothing manufacturing. A contract lawyer, he had studied art history as a young man and had maintained his curiosity and his knowledge. Allen was genuinely interested in the endeavors of the faculty and could carry on educated, insightful conversations about art. Allen and Amanda had recently moved from an old Providence mansion after their daughters headed off to college. Their new "smaller" home was the top floor of a converted warehouse in the jewelry district.

The living space was enormous, encompassing the whole width of the narrow building, which meant windows on both sides. The ceiling was rough old wood, original varnish yellowed with age, and exposed ductwork painted flat black. The exterior walls were exposed brick and the floor newly finished, unstained wide plank oak. Around a large rustic stone fireplace was the only carpeted area, one with deep, cozy seating. The area rug looked to be an oversized authentic antique Persian with a hunting motif. Woven in pale rose, beige, and a still intensely deep navy. Meant to be "read" from the bottom up, a tree spread its branches, an asp-like dragon wrapped around the trunk. The foliage supported the scattered hunters and hunted. Graceful antelope, leopards, and fowl eluded hunters on horseback with dagger or bow at the ready. The border depicted prey being plundered and eaten by predators. The tree of life; the deaths from predators, be it man or beast. I thought of Thomas and how similar humankind's place in this world is from the scene before me. Almost as though the negative space in the depiction was left for people. We are depredated, consumed. Not to fulfill biological hunger, but a hunger none the less. It was the most extraordinary Persian I'd ever seen. From what I know about antique rugs, I'd estimate it was worth more than the price of the loft and its renovations added together.

Nooks along the inner walls were nestled in spaces that were not always visible, depending on where I stood. A wall would almost invisibly be in front of another, lit so that from a small distance it looked to be on the same plane. The nooks held small bookshelves, a chair, perhaps a little desk. One corner held a baby grand piano at which a woman sat playing jazz. The kitchen was open to the whole area. Built with pale wood and stainless steel, it was intentionally subdued by its surroundings. From the near floor-to-ceiling windows, the lights of Providence blinked at us below. I wandered around the amazing space in awe.

These parties were a rare chance to visit with my colleagues without the oftentimes strident demands of students. I genuinely liked most of the instructors. They were hard working, dedicated, and enthusiastic, and kept their artistic egos in check. Most of them anyway. Andrew Pearson was the exception. Regardless of where we were, what we were doing: in the office, at an opening, in the street, he found a way to needle me either by shamelessly pointing out his many shows, always in SOHO (or so he said), or asking me where I was showing, or wondering aloud if I'd ever start writing again. Some of his comments were mildly homophobic. Phrases including "choice" or "lifestyle" put my teeth on edge, not to mention his oblique references to sin and sinners. There was no clear clue as to why he didn't like me personally. Ah, well, I didn't particularly like him either.

Allen Kindrick cornered me at one point, and we spent nearly an hour talking about the series I was doing. His interest was in the history of how the female nude is viewed compared with the male. We talked about the social implications: women sexualized by the male gaze and the power differential inherent in heterosexuality. I told him my interest in painting male nudes was because I preferred their bodies. He laughed. But then we talked about the ways in which the sexual aspect was vital, because it was with me, and how it continued to be different for women painted by men, the outsider—the painter—always looking at a mystery, an intrinsic unfamiliarity with a body. We agreed that it was partly a consequence of heterosexuality in not ever truly *knowing* the object of one's desire, nor being particularly interested in the knowledge. I talked about how, when I look at men, I also see myself, and how that makes it harder, for me anyway, to objectify whom I desire. He asked me about style. Mine is heavy-handed impasto. I do underpainting, but only in consideration of my sgraffito, the scratching down to the canvas, not necessarily in deference to the subject. It is more of a color consideration.

Late in the evening, after I'd stuffed myself full of rich canapes and overindulged on their expensive liquor, I was leaning against a bookshelf half hidden in a nook, taking some weight off my aching leg when Pearson approached. I had rather managed to avoid him throughout the evening until now. This year he brought his disagreeable wife who hadn't smiled for the entire evening. I could see why he strayed. But not why he didn't divorce.

Earlier Rita and I had sat by the fire to rest our feet. She knew enough people here to keep herself entertained; besides, she was a social worker, and people's stories were her nectar. "But, who is that woman in the horrible teal?" Well, she could be a little, erm, "analytical," but I loved that about her. The woman in question was Pearson's wife. "Well. She doesn't like you much. She was asking me about Thomas and your involvement." Rita said that Marge thought the "scandal" of his murder portrayed the department as some sort of Sodom and Gomorrah. Rita allowed as those were her own words, not Marge's, and I chuckled at the entitlement. She said Marge had spoken as though we had control over when bad things happen to us. As though Thomas had asked for it. Sinfulness equals murder. Sinfulness equals infections. Gah! My leg itched.

"So, I hear there's trouble in gaydom," Pearson said with a smirk, stopping aggressively right in front of me.

"Huh?" I am known for my witty repartee. Truthfully, I was pleasantly drunk, in a mellow mood, enjoying the hell out of the piano music, and I did not particularly want to engage.

"Thomas. You. Murder," dramatically stressing the horrible act like it was written in a mystery novel. *Murrderrr*. Ass.

"Jesus, Pearson. Have some respect. He was just a kid." My tone tetchy.

"Thomas was a rampant whore," Andrew threw back.

"What the fuck?"

"Sure. I heard it around. He'd been treated for syphilis a couple of times, you know." He looked me in the eyes as if I really did or should know.

Andrew Pearson was a tenured photography professor. He was brilliant in the darkroom, his technical skills were as obsessive as Ansel Adams, whom he purportedly hated. Pearson could handle computer technology exceptionally well, having learned the old technologies that had come out decades ago, and keeping abreast of the newest. He was nearing sixty by now, I guessed. I thought his subject matter kind of exploitive on a few levels. I think he used women's bodies with a lack of depth or candor, respect, maybe, and he mimicked Mapplethorpe's style without shame. Not the S&M per se, but the lighting and contrast along with some contorted poses. For me, it was all slightly pornographic, unlike Mapplethorpe's intentional provocativeness. But he must have a good rep who cleverly markets him because he sells. Andrew, for the nearly thirty years he'd been at RISD, chose a female junior or senior for a lover—one who usually lasted a year or two. Remarkably he never got called out on it, not once. He was an incredibly handsome man with perfectly salted black hair and an athletic build. He reminded me of Clooney but more severe, less boyish. I could see why the young women fell, acquiesced, pursued, whatever. The current paramour was a gorgeous, tall, volatile Russian with Slavic high cheekbones, fine ash-colored hair. He'd started the affair in her junior year, and it had continued into the next. I'd had her in a few classes. She was sharp and contrary, negotiating grades, assignments, homework... Potentially fiery in bed I supposed, if you marched that way, but almost certainly difficult.

"That's bullshit. How on earth would you even know that?"

"Well, the nurse was a very talkative young woman as she didn't smoke." A self-satisfied smile tugged at the outer corners of his thin lips. He not only cheated on his wife, but he'd cheat on his girlfriends too, apparently.

"Christ Pearson, is there anyone you *haven't* sleep with?" The man made me bristle.

He paused the perfected beat. "You, darling." He met my eyes for only an instant. I didn't know whether to laugh or clock him, but the decision was made for me. He turned and strutted off. As I tried to unfreeze my thoughts, one was immediate: Andrew Pearson slept with men.

And, Andrew Pearson's wife did not like him talking to me. As he walked off, I saw her over his shoulder, and the look she gave me cried repugnance. I had the urge to yell to her that I was not the one sleeping with every human (one could only hope) that came his way. Instead, I shook off the weird exchange and headed toward the piano, pouring a last two fingers of scotch.

How deep is the ocean?
How high is the sky?

As the end of the night approached, my wrecked mellow mood turned more thoughtful. Rita headed over and put her arm through mine as I leaned against the baby grand. "Looking a little pensive, Start."

I thought I was probably feeling too many things to even begin to sort out, but pensive was close enough.

How many times in a day
Do I think of you?

"Rita." I sighed. "How do you give up obsessing over something you don't have? Can't have?" I turned to look out toward the river and the lights along the far bank. The cold air off the water seemed to make the lights brittle, pointed. Hearing a similar laugh in the background I thought of the first time I heard Jake laugh. He laughed, every time, as though he'd never expected to ever laugh. Each time like it was a surprise. I wondered if I'd ever hear it again.

How far would I travel
To be where you are

How far is the journey
From here to a star
And if I ever lost you
How much would I cry
How deep is the ocean
How high is the sky

Suddenly I was spent. I felt the scrape of an unrequited desire, like a palette knife searching for the canvas. Downing my last swallow, I turned to Rita. "Let's go home."

*

I spent Sunday lying low. Rita came by for our morning ritual, not talking much, our combined hangovers an effective mute. The rest of the day I spent reading the newspaper and then reading a new Julian Barnes. The aftermath of the night of drink had me feeling a little melancholy, but mostly I just felt uneasy. When Monday finally came, at least I had something potentially productive to do.

Addams of Addams Property Management turned out to be a McAllister who was short and round and bald with the conversational skills of a fish. He let me into Thomas's apartment with only a warning not to take anything. The man said he wasn't going to wait around and asked that I engage the doorknob lock, and he'd come back to lock the deadbolt later. He also warned that he'd had people in to clean up some, but they were coming back after he emptied the apartment. He still had to replace the carpet and paint. Suddenly I wasn't sure I'd made the right decision coming here. I wasn't ready to face the magnitude of what had happened, but the guy was standing there with the door open, waiting for me to go in, so I did.

The first thing I looked for was the computer that was the source of my immediate trouble. But it was gone, of course. The police would have taken it. The empty computer desk was against the far wall, and the only other furnishings in the room were a bank of plain unfinished wooden bookcases, a futon under a large window, and a dated, somewhat grubby armchair. The rest of the room was full of cheap taborets and plastic bins crammed with art supplies, an easel, and canvases. There were stacks of drawings everywhere, and illustrations and drawings were pinned and taped to the walls. The artwork around the computer table had been removed, the outlines shown by a few spatters of blood, now the color of burnt umber, and the ecru carpet had translucent puce stains, indicating some scrubbing, in a variety of sizes and shapes. But one very large one where Thomas's head must have lain. Not much cleaning done otherwise, but no tissue or gray matter.

Being there, in his apartment, the crime seemed more graphic, making the act itself, what Thomas might have felt or thought, more immediate and tangible. Did he know he was going to die? Was it a surprise? Did he never know? I hoped it didn't hurt. I hoped he wasn't afraid. I hoped he left life feeling as though he'd added something to someone else's life somewhere, that he had value. But he probably didn't have a chance to think at all. And he was so young. Do the young add value in this moment? To whom? Or do we have to wait around for bigger, better accomplishments before we tally importance? Is it history that creates the bulk and depth of value? He was so young. He was potential cut short. What does that mean? Half a letter? Half a word? Half a meaning? There is nothing real in "potential." Who would mourn him, truly weep, sob, tear at their hair, their clothes, despair in their loss? I had not thought of these things this profoundly until now, and I felt like a selfish, narcissistic prick, pining over Jake, worrying about my writing, bleating about my leg. I should have been caring about this; this boy, this horrible, senseless loss. I sat on the futon and scrunched my fists into my eyes. *You can do one thing, Start: try to figure out what happened to this kid.* That's how I'd honor him. Not in how I'd failed him but in knowing, and having someone who knows carry on, remember him, speak of him from time to time.

I rose and began looking aimlessly through the piles of drawings, the stacks of canvases. Faces and bodies of familiar RISD models, and some I didn't know. Was that important? Was there information encoded in the unfamiliar? I eventually wandered over to the bookcases. Mostly art and illustration books. Some fiction, popular stuff, but some classics, some poetry. One of my slight volumes brought a sad smile. I crouched and pulled an old well-yellowed *Anatomy for the Artist* from the bottom shelf. I had one just like it. I opened it, and a bookmark floated out, landing at the point where two bookcases were almost butted next to each other but for a gap of a couple of inches. As I picked it up, I glanced between the two cases. Something was back there. I pulled my phone out of my coat pocket and turned on the flashlight. I could see the color of cardboard. As I stood, the gap grew narrower, and by the time I was erect, the bookcases were fully met. I went to the side to look behind it. A thin cardboard portfolio was barely visible in the tight space. I could, only just, prize it out with a finger that I had to keep licking in order for it not to slip off the smooth tan paper.

When I opened the folder, sweat broke out on my forehead and my hands began to shake. *Son of a bitch. I should not have come.* The images were beautiful. Sheet after sheet of newsprint, fine drawing paper, typing paper, heavy, cold press watercolor paper, all of the same man. Nudes, portraits, gesture drawings, studies. Some in charcoal, some in beautifully hued soft pastels, some pencil drawings, watercolors, gouache. Some were obviously posed, some looked like the subject was unaware, all rendered with such care, such...adoration. I did not want to see these pictures. In that instant, I was furious at Thomas for challenging the way I saw him, thought of him. Andrew Pearson's intent gaze stared back.

"Fuck. Me," I said aloud. I started to put the folder back. My instinct was to protect Thomas from scandal, at worst, mockery, at best. I chuckled bitterly. *He's dead, you ass.* I had to tell the police. They obviously needed to know about this find. Or did they? Was the content even connected to anything? I started looking in earnest for other "hidden gems." Opening a closet, I came across all of his class portfolios, and I wondered what the detectives had made of the faces and bodies contained within this little space that was Thomas's home. They were on the walls, in folders, piled on the floor, stuffed in the closet. Did they know what to look for, who to look for? I was even one of the faces left on the wall. I recognized it. It was from a class where the model didn't show, so I'd posed, clothed of course, for the students and let them draw me. Did that add to the detectives' suspicions? There was no way around it, the hidden portfolio meant something. It was a thing I didn't want to have to deal with. Despite my dislike of Pearson, or because of it, I did not want him to be involved in this cockup. But I had come here to find something, and I did. I had to tell the detectives.

My initial thought was how to avoid talking to Jake. Calling Ransom was the obvious choice, of course, but I knew there would be a little...well, probably a lot, said about my poking around here, and in a way, Ransom was scarier than Jake. Although, since it was no longer an official crime scene, there was little they could do about it except suspect me more. I remembered that the receipt Jake had asked me to sign and send back was still sitting in my car in a stampless envelope. Who on earth has a bleeding stamp these days? On impulse, I decided to drive over to the police station. I'd ask for Ransom, and if he wasn't around, I'd drop the receipt off and call him from home.

Interstate 95 cuts an ugly swath through Providence, dividing Federal Hill, where the station is, from downtown. It also makes it a pain to get to. The station itself is in what's called the Providence Public Safety Complex which houses both the police and the fire department as well as Providence homeland security. The complex is but a combination of two old brick office buildings united by a cement affair stuck to their backs, and a glass boat-shaped atrium added between to join them. I found a spot in the lot and limped in. I identified myself at the information desk and asked for Detective Ransom. The receptionist dialed a number, asked for Ransom and stated my name. She looked up and asked me what it was in regards to. I answered that it was about Thomas Wilson. She relayed the information. After hanging up, she directed me to a set of chairs and requested I have a seat.

It is not true that stations are full of criminals being manhandled by police as they wend their way to the cells, or whatever. At least not in Providence. It was mostly just people waiting. They were standing around, laughing, talking, coming, going, shushing children, waiting. Maybe it was only a peaceful lull in the day. I was unfamiliar with the building, having never been in it, and therefore, didn't know where to look for Ransom. I let my gaze wander. I was standing near the chairs watching a mother talking earnestly with a young boy, so only saw someone come up to my side out of the corner of my eye.

"Ian," Jake said. I don't know how a heart can skip a beat, drop at the same time, and still leave a man upright, but it happened.

"Oh, Jake. I was looking for Detective Ransom, actually," I said coolly.

"He's not here. What's up?" Bland elocution, bland expression. Well, what should I have expected?

"Ah, yes. I should have called first." I hesitated. I was not sure I wanted to talk to Jake about what I'd found. I knew where I stood with Ransom, at least. I was not sure I wanted to know where I stood with Jake. Well, I supposed I knew, but it was easier not actually hearing it. Leave me *some* fantasy wiggle room. But here I was, best to just get it out and over with. "Look, I've come across something I think you should know about."

Jake looked at me evenly and nodded. "Okay. Let's go up to my desk." We headed back to the info desk, and he got me a visitor's pass. I watched his strong fingers clip it on to my coat lapel. I found it an oddly intimate gesture. He motioned me to follow him, and we headed up a set of stairs to the second floor and then along a short hallway into a large room with several desks, some face-to-face. This scene was sort of like TV. The area was messy with papers, Styrofoam coffee cups, takeout boxes, and noisy, with ringing phones and chatter. A few civilian-looking people were in serious conversations with other, I assumed, detectives who were all dressed alike in sports coats, button-down shirts, and ties. A sea of gray and navy with an occasional brown. Jake led me toward the back, nearer the windows. It was late afternoon, and the sun was on the other side of the building, casting the white walls in a cold-blue light. The omnipresent overhead fluorescent lighting hummed and popped and blinked. It would give me a headache soon.

He sat at his desk, leaving the obligatory chair at the side for me. I sat, nervous, scratching at my knuckles. Again, he asked, "What's up?"

What I related to him was this: that I had gone to Thomas's apartment today and found the portfolio, that I'd left it there. Then I told him about what was in the collection. I told him about the weird comment that Pearson had made Saturday night about Thomas's sex work (not the one about Pearson not sleeping with me). I said that Justin had related something similar to Jen, but now Justin was missing. Jake listened patiently, still with this incredibly flat expression that was making me increasingly uneasy, agitated.

When I was done, he swiveled his chair to face me, leaned in, put his hand on the desk, and said, "Ian. Considering the fact that you continue to be, shall we say 'a person of interest' in this case, how on earth could you be so stupid as to go back to what was the fucking crime scene?" His tone was sharp, starting at a reasonable volume but rising as he finished.

Well, there you have it, Start. "Go back?" It came out a little louder than I'd intended, but the volume of it felt right, reinforced my indignity. I, too, leaned in and said quietly, in a tone of disbelief, "You think I did it." I realized

I hadn't fully believed that he thought so, or I'd held out hope until this instant.

"I didn't say that. I didn't mean *back*."

"Here's the thing that gets me, Jake," I said tightly, still leaning in. "You know me. And by 'know me,' I mean more than that we have had our dicks in each other's asses. And you're sitting there believing there is even a remote possibility that I could have done it." I was practically hissing, which is not necessarily quiet. A few detectives turned our way. I knew I was siphoning the hurt I felt that Jake had opted not to believe in my innocence to anger—there, you see how well buried hope can be?—and the hurt was more profound than I'd known. I stood. Grabbed my cane.

Jake stood then too. I could feel his breath. Hot, smelling of coffee and cinnamon, he was inches from my face. "Yeah, right. I know you. I know that after six months..." He stopped, took a breath, put his mouth next to my ear and growled, "I fell in love with you, Ian. You knew it. And you shut that door like it was...nothing. That's the you I know." He stepped back and sat down. "Thanks for letting us know about these 'developments,' Ian." Sarcasm sucks as a communication strategy.

I stood at the side of his desk, literally huffing. I'm sure my face was that horrible streaky blush, but today I didn't give a shit. And I was done whispering. I did not care who heard. I said tautly, but conversationally, "Just so I have this straight; you are equating the ability, my ability, to break your heart with the ability to murder someone." Jake stared at papers on his desk. A frown of fake concentration on his face. Silence. "Got it." I turned and started to walk off, throwing over my shoulder: "Fuck you, Jake."

A few steps more and I heard a hint of apology in, "Ian."

I stopped and turned and waited. He was standing at his desk looking at me. Nothing. "Fuck. You." I certainly said that so he could hear me. Detectives and their victims had all stopped to look at us, and now they looked at me. Whatever. Turning again, I walked away.

I was furious. My vision tunneled, the periphery black, my center vision bathed in red, and I could not get out of that building fast enough. If I could run, I would have. I employed the fastest possible walk. Once outside, the cold late afternoon darkness helped diffuse the heat in my face so by the time I reached my car I was at least safe to drive. I stuck my hand in my coat pocket for my keys and felt the envelope with the receipt in it. I snorted, pulled it out, and threw it over my shoulder.

Chapter Eight

By the time I got home, I was still in a rage. I parked in my drive, down nearer the street, and went in the front door, slamming it shut as I flung my coat half-assed toward a chair and stomped up to my studio. Within minutes, I'd poured my scotch, turned music on loud enough to fill the house, grabbed my palette and began flinging the paint at the canvas. Eventually, I felt the familiar pull of the detachment, so I gladly let go.

So gone was I that when I felt a hand on my shoulder the fright was so visceral I threw my arms up, stepped away awkwardly, on my left leg, which gave beneath me, and I crumpled, taking my pallet, my scotch, and my jar of turpentine with me, letting out a half swallowed scream. My heart was unquestionably on its way to win a race without me, and I instinctively threw an arm over my face.

I came back from wherever I had been, finding some focus in the pain radiating from my leg. Jake was crouched in front of me, his hand extended but not touching me, insistently repeating my name, "Ian... Ian... Ian."

I lay the rest of the way back with a groan, feeling a wet puddle soaking into my shirt, an arresting odor emanating from the unusual combination of solvents: scotch and turpentine. I slowly unfolded my leg. "What the hell are you doing in my house?" I shouted to the ceiling, all the fury returning in a rush. I started to sit up, checking other body parts along the way.

"I knocked, rang the bell, called your cell phone. I could hear the music and see lights on. I got worried and tried the door. It wasn't locked. I called your name all the way up the stairs. You didn't hear me?"

I stood, using a tall stool for leverage. Jake tried to help, but I shook him off. I was still angry, and now he lets himself into my home? Ignoring his question, I rephrased mine. "What do you want?" To avoid getting sucked into that cerulean vortex, I didn't meet his eyes. Instead, I stripped off my stinking, sopping shirt and threw it in a corner.

"You, okay? Maybe you should sit down, Ian." His voice carried a familiar gentleness. As I stumbled toward my little sofa, the affair with Jake, that whole summer, replayed in the bizarre manner of memory. It can run through time at such speed...yet recollections feel neither stilled nor fast-forwarded. The realization came as quickly; he was right, I had been a prick to him. I shut the door the minute Arty was back. I told myself at the time that I'd been honest with Jake regarding Arty, and I had been. But I hadn't been honest with myself. Isn't that what we neglect when we say, "But I was always honest with you"? If we utter the words, we believe we absolve ourselves of the consequences to others. I recalled the recent hurt in his voice after I told him that Arty was no longer in my life, and he'd asked why I hadn't called him. He thought it was because I hadn't wanted to. He didn't know it was because I was missing the part of myself that would have allowed it.

I sat and closed my eyes, waiting for the scarred adhesions to settle back to their regular spots. "I'm okay.

A minute, all right?" Jake nodded and sat across from me, arms on thighs, watching me intently.

After a good minute, after my breathing slowed, Jake spoke softly. "I'm sorry for what I said, Ian. I don't think you had anything to do with it. I don't know why I said that." He waited for a response. If he thought I was going to let myself off that easy, he was nuts. I didn't want to deflect what Jake needed to say, and I needed to hear it. I remained silent for once. We gazed at each other, each in our own heads. "I was angry, I guess." He finally ventured. I nodded. Waited. "I know you told me how it was with you and Arty, and I thought I could handle it." He looked away and took a breath as if planning to go on. On an exhale, he merely shook his head. *The loss is trust,* I thought. Maybe all feelings of loss are tied to trust.

"No..." I yielded the last of my anger. "No. I knew how you felt. You know, I thought then I was taking the...what? The 'chosen' path, I suppose. It was the understanding Arty and I had. I didn't know I could change my mind. That I should have." He looked at me, and it was then I was caught in that cerulean maelstrom, inextricably. "Jake," I muttered.

And he was there, in front of me with my face in his hands, pulling me toward that soft, beautiful mouth. I bent forward, and we pressed lips together tenderly, chastely, feeling each other's breath on our cheeks. My hands slid up his sides, under his arms to his back, finding the bottom of his sharp shoulder blades. I pulled him in and parted my knees as he knelt on the floor in front of me. He drew away only enough to open his mouth, his tongue flicking my upper lip like a knock at a door. They met; the kiss deepened, moved from gentle exploratory twists and nudges to a needful sucking, plunges, and nips as we parted and reunited. The wet smacking and soft groans filled the silence. My cock had long since filled the empty fold of my pants created by sitting. I wanted this man.

Demons hide in familiar places, yet we never think to look for them before venturing out. As Jake's hands moved down my sides, heading past my waist to my legs, Satan roared. I grabbed his arms and shoved myself back into the depths of the sofa. "Wait, wait," I gasped. Jake sat back on his heels and looked at me expectantly. Okay. Now what? "Jake, this is probably not such a good idea, is it? I mean with your job and my, um, position, being a suspect and all. I wouldn't want you to lose your job." Yeah, that was coherent.

He quirked a smile at me. "Well, I wouldn't be announcing it to anyone. Besides—" Shit. I was going to do it again. Hurt him. Hurt us both. I stood, nearly knocking him on his ass. He reached back with his arm to leverage his too perfect body away and up, rising also.

"Jake," I interrupted, "I'm kind of...broken right now. I know how weak that sounds. Maybe it is. But to get you, especially you, involved in my, my...shit, I can't...*won't* do it. I'm sorry. I'm...sorry." I turned to head down the stairs when he grabbed my arm.

"You could talk to me. I could make that decision," he said with the voice of reason.

"I know. But you'd choose to try because you're a kind, big-hearted fella, who would not want to hurt someone over this kind of mess. Nope. Trust me. Go home, Jake."

Jake took a long moment to look at me. His expression was at first disbelieving but transformed to angry. *Better angry belief than calm disbelief.* "Huh. Okay. Sure. And to use *your* famous words: fuck you, Ian.

Fuck. You." With that, he moved around me and nearly hurled himself down the stairs. I was still standing at the top when I heard the front door slam.

*

It had been a long time since I couldn't get out of bed. I spent two days under the comforter. I got up to drink water, pee, feed the cat. I stank. I didn't give a shit. The phone rang. I didn't answer. On day three I heard Rita calling up the stairs. I didn't care. Well, I did when she ripped the comforter off me. But only marginally. I was in boxers, so she wasn't horribly shocked by my nakedness. However, my leg was exposed, partially anyway. Rita had never seen it. No one had seen it except my doctors, physical therapists, my mother, and Arty.

"Get up, Ian. Go take a shower. I'll meet you downstairs." I pulled the comforter back up. "Really, Ian! Get up!"

"I'm okay, Rita. Go home." I said in a reassuring tone that must have sounded pathetic because she didn't go home.

"Ian. I have been as empathetic, nurturing, cajoling, kind, patient, and loving as I could be with you and your injuries, physical and otherwise. But I've had it. I'm done." She pulled the comforter completely off the bed.

I rolled onto my back and looked up at her bleakly. "I know, Rita. You've been the best of friends to me. I kind of knew I would burn you out eventually. But I'll be okay. Don't worry. Go home." *Jesus, I am a fucking parody of myself.*

"Yeah, no. I'm not leaving, asshole, I'm changing tactics. Get the fuck up." I wasn't sure I was liking this tactic or this Rita.

"Rita. Frankly, I don't give a damn about your tactics or if you stay or go. I am exactly where I want to be. I do *not* want to get up. I do *not* want to fulfill your fantasy of who I am or who I could be." That was laid on with a heavy-handed and unmistakable jab at the psychotherapy I had consistently refused. "I do not want to fulfill anyone's fantasy, desire, need, want...anything. I want to be left alone."

Rita bent over me, her face inches from mine and spat, "Get up you little shit, or I will dump cold water on you and your narcissistic little ass until your balls freeze off." I stared at her. She stared back. I sighed dramatically and sat up. "Shower. You reek." She turned and headed down the stairs. I seriously considered lying back down, but that just meant the whole exchange would go on repeat, like Bill Murray in *Groundhog Day*. I snorted derisively at myself and headed for the shower.

She was sitting at my kitchen table when I came down. Two cups of coffee, her hands around one as if warming herself. I slumped into a chair, undried hair dripping into my cup, and sipped morosely, not making eye contact. I wasn't embarrassed by my behavior. I knew I should have been. I just did not want to engage. The late afternoon sun was casting a pink glow, turning the white of the walls the palest salmon.

"What happened, Ian? And don't say 'nothing.' Don't lie, deflect, distract, avoid, minimize, or shut down. For once, just talk to me. Nothing bad will happen. I promise." It occurred to me that I didn't deserve the gentleness people offered. I used to be a nice person. I'm not anymore. I don't know what I am, but it's not nice.

"Jake came over. He wanted, well, we wanted... And then I couldn't. I got scared, started to panic. I'm not ready for Jake. I want him, but he's too much. That sounds so trite when I hear it out loud. I'm not getting at what I mean." I scrubbed up and down my face and ran my fingers through my damp hair.

"Why is he too much?"

"Mmm..." I shook my head, trying to find words. "It feels like he just fills up my head. He's too intense, loyal. Loyal to a fault. I think he'd get in over his head with me and be too, I don't know, too fine of a person to say '*Ish*, what a fucking mess, what a fucking mistake,' and go. He'd just stay and end up hating me."

"Hmm. Different from Arty, who did exactly that: say *ish* and go. You'd prefer that." Not a question. A challenge.

"I understood it."

"You wouldn't understand if someone chose to stay." A statement.

A long pause. Then the truth. "No."

"Because..." She waited.

"It wouldn't be worth it."

"It? What is it?"

"I don't know; the relationship, the trouble, *me*, I guess."

"How do you judge a worth of a man, Ian? What makes a man worthy?"

"I don't know, wholeness."

"Integrity," she construed. "Go on."

"Strength, maybe."

"Like the ability to surmount some terrible odds?"

I saw where she was going. I sat back. "Now I think you're just being clever, Rita."

"I don't see it that way. I think you *are* scared, and I think you've talked and thought and drunk your way into this pit of fearful self-loathing. That just makes me sad,

Ian. You have so much in you to love and respect and rely on that the flaws, which we all have, should become small and manageable. But they don't because you pick at them, keep them open and oozing so they're real but unhealed and, as a result, always at the forefront. But those few people you've let partway in—me, Fredrick—we see the other stuff. We've peeked around your battered corners. We haven't run."

"No. But I think you said it. 'Partway in.' All the way in is different. Others have seen all the way in and ran. Arty ran." I could not imagine how it would feel to have Jake run. I could let Arty go, but not Jake. Why? "Arty wasn't all the way in though," I said and looked up at Rita. She met my gaze evenly.

"No? How not?"

"No. I could never let Arty all the way in. *He* wasn't all the way in. I was never enough for him." I'd never thought of it that way. "I always just thought it was our agreement. I agreed to it so it must have been 'ours.' But I didn't really agree to it, I accepted it. Is that different from agreeing?"

"Maybe. It feels different though, huh?" she asked. I nodded in response.

I stood to pour another cup of coffee. "Jake would want all the way in. He wanted in back then. He'll want in now. I don't think he'll know what he's getting into. I have panic attacks, I drink too much, I can disappear on myself, I have night terrors, and I have flashbacks. How could I possibly ask anyone in? It's too crowded." I sat back down.

"What does he see in you?" I looked at her face for the sarcasm that wasn't in her tone. It wasn't there. It was an honest question.

"I haven't the foggiest. Truly. I was a poet once. Maybe he thinks that man still exists. Maybe what he wants now doesn't exist anymore."

"I happen to think that we are always everything that we have ever been."

"Very Zen." I sat again with my coffee.

She shrugged. "Gotta be something." She smiled a little. "Ian, I'm gonna sound clichéd when I say this, but there is a lot of truth in clichés. We are all flawed. We are all injured. Some have bigger flaws, greater injuries than others, but we all deserve to be loved. There are people out there who see injuries and flaws as the weft and the warp of an interesting person. You've run into some men, Arty, who have too little imagination. You have to find out where people fit with you. You can't just make assumptions. You have to figure it out."

"You don't think I've lost some critical thing? I feel like I have."

"Not really. I think it's all still there. Under a bunch of scar tissue."

I nodded, not sure if I agreed, but I wanted to believe what she said. Looking into my coffee, I felt the tears come, but they felt a little different this time. "Thanks, Rita."

She stood up, kissed the top of my head, ruffled my hair. "Change your locks, Ian. And don't go back to bed," she said as she headed out the back door. I stared into my cup until the coffee cooled.

*

I didn't go back to bed. Classes started next week. I went up to my den and booted up the laptop. The top floor still stank of turps and scotch. I dropped a stack of newspaper on top of the stain to staunch the wafting odor. I downloaded my class schedule for the next semester. Two classes of upper-level drawing. That was perfect for me. Ever since my injury, I stopped wanting to be a full-time instructor. I was fully qualified, having a double master's in fine art and English and a doctorate in creative writing, but I found the politics, the blinders worn by the administration, and the departmental infighting of academia stultifying. The less it applied to me the happier I was. I just wanted to teach. I don't know how tenured professors, weighed under by the poor wage, the oblivious administration, and the restrictive educational philosophies imposed on imaginative teachers, could endure year after year and still have something to offer. But some do persevere. Some end up bitter and unbending. I was lucky in my financial situation not to have to test myself.

After talking to Rita, I felt a little lighter. Not happier, but less burdened anyway. I swiveled my chair to the side and put my feet up on the windowsill. I didn't have much of a view. A tall brick structure across the street, a little view to the side, some homes with slivers for front yards, nicely planted with what they call 'winter interest.' Sometimes, while I sat there, a bird, a pigeon, an odd gull would bravely land on my wide window ledge. I squinted as the sunlight hit me, thinking. When had I ever laid myself out for anyone? I thought I had with Arty, back before the damage. But I hadn't. Had I always been closed off? I knew I was now. I attributed it to the injury, the sequela. It had become my reason, my defense, my wall, my mantra. Now I felt like I was at the edge of a cliff, blindly stepping off, hoping there would be something substantial to step onto. Not a man of faith, I had nothing to base my next action on but hope. I picked up the phone and dialed his number.

I don't like the phone, and 90 percent of the time when I make calls, I hope for voice mail. Today I wanted him to answer. Of course, it went to voice mail. "Jake, it's Ian. You may not want to talk to me, and I wouldn't blame you, really. But I want to talk to you about what happened. Why I do... Why I say the shit I do... I...well, call me, if you would, Jake." I clicked off.

Chapter Nine

I spent some time cleaning up my studio. Not much to do with the stain but to apply more solvent, sop it up, and neutralize it with detergent. I'd not refinished the floors up here intentionally, letting the paint and drips fall where they may without worry. There was history to the splatters and smears. I looked at the painting I'd been working on when Jake came. The dog again, with its back to the viewer, and a boy in the background with something menacing in his hand. The paint was thick, laid on with a palette knife adding painterly depth, dimension. It was me. My work, style. It wasn't as though I didn't recognize it, but it felt remote, like something from somewhere inaccessible. Not for the first time, I wondered about my sanity.

Jake didn't call that day, nor the next, although I don't know why I thought he might. I tried to keep busy. Fredrick and I went out for dinner one night, choosing Italian on Federal Hill, Pane e Vino. We'd ordered a bottle of Ripassa Valpolicella Superiore. We went full out with splitting an antipasto and a *primi*: fritto misto, and lobster ravioli. We went our separate ways for the *secondi*. I chose a wood-grilled pork chop; Fredrick had scallops. It was rich and indulgent and improved my mood. The restaurant was crowded and noisy with laughter, clinking glasses, dropped plates, happy din. It agreeably filled another evening where Jake didn't call.

At home, with evening ablutions completed, I crawled into bed with the Julian Barnes I had started and let his lovely turn of phrase lull me to blinks and heavy lids. Shutting off the light, I snuggled into the fluffy down and drifted off.

I dreamt of the dog.

I was on the cliff again, and the dog was in front of me, snarling and chewing on something in the navy and emerald grass of night. I wanted to see what it was, but it was as if I were glued to the ground. I could not lift either leg. I leaned over as far as I could to see without getting snapped at. I could...just...barely...see.

The scream I was unable to realize in my dream caught in my throat as I sat up suddenly, disoriented, sweating. The bone the dog had been chewing had been my leg.

And Rita wants me to put myself out there!

*

Classes started and still no call from Jake. My thoughts were circular: concern that he was sick or injured, anger that he couldn't just pick up the phone, resignation that he was not interested, concern...

I wondered what the detectives had made of the information I'd given Jake. Surely they'd gone back to Thomas's apartment to look at the portfolio. It had been intentionally hidden. Why? Scenarios popped into my head like a slide show. For some reason, I believed Pearson had something to do with what happened to Thomas. While I couldn't quite slot him in as the killer, I could see him as having triggered the event. But the how eluded me. A jealous lover on either side, maybe? I didn't have details, and the possibility of getting any from the police seemed beyond remote. But there were some clues in the questions they'd asked, like Thomas being injured by someone. Did Pearson do that? Or someone else, someone he'd had sex with—a customer? I definitely wanted to talk to Pearson, but I wasn't sure I wanted to hear what the man had to say. He'd seemed so spiteful of Thomas at the party, yet there was apparently some kind of intimacy there at one time. The thought sort of nauseated me.

Jen had still not heard from Justin. She'd found out he was scheduled this semester but had not attended his first classes. None of his friends had heard from him either, but they seemed less concerned than both Jen and me. Maybe it was this sinister mist shrouding our views that had us thinking the worst regarding Justin.

I asked Jen about Pearson's schedule. I was on my way out, but I might wait for him if he was in today. She said he'd probably be in the office in an hour. That would work. I spent the time thinking about Jake. I contemplated going by the station but didn't anticipate that going over well after our scene. I could go by his apartment, but I realized I didn't know where he lived. Actually, I didn't know anything about his current personal life, did I? And I'm fantasizing about waltzing back into it? Idiocy. I pulled out my phone and searched his name. The search app had three pages of Jake Quinns in Providence. I started thumbing through them looking for one that had Brockton listed as a prior residence. I finally found a match, but it recorded a Christian Mayes as a relative or associated person. The name did not ring a bell. I knew that the information on these pages are notoriously inaccurate, so I didn't pay much attention. Of course, nothing is free, so I coughed up the few bucks it took to obtain an address. It was on South Angell St. in the Wayland neighborhood. I saved the address to my phone, then putzed around with paperwork until I heard Pearson's voice down the hall.

I left my office to lean against the wall next to his door. I didn't know what had happened after I told Jake about the portfolio; if the detectives had spoken with Pearson, or if my name had come up. I felt a little blind. Maybe I hadn't thought this confrontation (as I expected it would be) through. Pearson saw me and his expression changed from his usual smirk to one of annoyance. Okay. That was kind of normal.

"What's up, Start?" he said.

"I'd like to talk to you for a few minutes." I tried to keep my voice light. I didn't want to spook him.

"About what?" Now a little suspicious.

I nodded my head toward his door. "In your office?"

He shrugged, unlocked the door, and we went in. I closed the door after us. Like all art teachers' offices, it was crammed with student artwork, books, papers, chaos. He tossed his jacket, some long leather affair, over the only visitor chair and sat at his desk. Right. I could stand.

"Look," I started, "I'm not going to moralize or anything, so don't get defensive. I'm just trying to figure out what was going on with Thomas Wilson that got him killed." Pearson started to say something, his face already reddening with fury. "Wait, let me finish. I saw the portfolio Thomas had of the drawings—"

This time he did interrupt. He stood and stepped toward me menacingly. "You son of a bitch! *You* called the cops!" Taking me completely by surprise, he grabbed the lapels of my coat, shoved me back against the door with a bang, and spat, "Listen to me, you fucking little faggot, stay the fuck out of my life, and leave my family alone, or I'll fucking kill you."

I'm not a strong man, but I had some height on him, and I knew how to break most holds. However, what I did was to just stand there until his rage died. He stepped back suddenly. I intended to go on to explain how I found the portfolio until what he said dawned on me. "I haven't bothered your family, Andrew. I don't even know your family," I said softly, mystified.

"Get out," he spat. I did.

Jen had her coat half on, gawking at me as I backed out, waiting for me to say something, her mouth hanging a little open. I shrugged. Frankly, I was more than a little shaken. It's not often I get threatened, much less manhandled.

"Jen, I might need a little help." She raised two cautious eyebrows. "C'mon. I'll walk you out." I didn't want Pearson to hear what I had to say. "Would you mind keeping your ears open when Pearson's here? Are you working when he's around?"

"Some. This sounds very intriguey. What went on in there? What am I listening for?"

"That"—I jerked my head to indicate the office—"had to do with Thomas. He knows something about it. I don't know what. But you have to keep this quiet, Jen. It might be important." I stopped to look at her, trying to convey some seriousness without scaring her. I was a little scared.

"Okay, Ian. Sure." We parted when we got outside, and I headed home in the dark. I needed to tell Jake about this confrontation. I thought it was important for him to know about Pearson's reaction. I decided that I'd get the car and drive over to his apartment, given he was not answering my calls or returning my messages—all one of them.

His address turned out to be a handsome older redbrick apartment building in a trendy neighborhood. He must be doing pretty well. I couldn't find any parking spots, though, and I drove around for a while before lucking out and finding one a block away on a side street, as someone pulled out. The entryway was wired for two-way communication with buzzer buttons next to the names. I found Jake's neatly typed in a nice font. I pressed. After a few seconds a disembodied voice came through the round perforated grill in front of me.

"Yes?" It didn't really sound like Jake, but the sound was most likely distorted.

"Jake? It's Ian." I hoped I wouldn't be left standing in silence.

"No... It's Chris. Hold on."

Right. Sure. Chris. Now I didn't know whether to walk away or wait it out. I stood there staring at the stupid speaker as if it would offer me an answer. Instead, the door behind me opened, and there was Jake.

"Jake. Sorry. I'm interrupting. No—look, this can wait." I was backing through the outer door, like I'd caught him *in flagrante* or something. But his look said it all. Not embarrassed, just sorry maybe, acknowledging that my assumption was accurate. "I just wanted to tell you something, but it can wait. I can wait."

I was out the door and turning away.

"Ian, stop." I did. "Look. Things are just a little complicated right now."

No. Jake should not have to explain anything to me. I was being intrusive and presumptive. He'd had a life. Has a life. "No, Jake. Really. It's okay. I'll call Ransom in the morning. He can fill you in. You have a good evening, yeah?" On that, I turned and walked away. As I reached the corner and turned to look back, he was still standing there in the halo of the porch light, watching.

Bloody hell. *What a mash-up.* I got to my car and started for home, but somehow ended up at the Wild Colonial where I proceeded to sample the decent variety of Irish and Scotch whiskeys. What the hell is happening? Had I misread Jake that badly? Despite the misunderstandings, the hurt feelings, the anger, and despite my insecurities, he'd felt available. I thought he felt available. The drunker I got, the more I realized I'd been so focused on my fucked-up mental state that I'd forgotten to do basic groundwork. Like asking, "Are you seeing anyone?" Typical. But he was the one who kissed me, for fuck's sake. After a few hours of pretty much nonstop sipping, watching the patrons play at being Irish, I was not focusing. At all. Mission accomplished. I was hammered. I called a cab to take me home, where I fell into bed and dreamless sleep.

Unfortunately, the idiocy of the previous night meant a hungover workday. I decided I would pretend that yesterday never happened. Maybe I'd act as though the last two months never happened. At any rate, I didn't call Ransom. Pearson was on the police radar, so to speak, which meant I could stay out of it. Or so I told myself. If I was being honest, I'd admit that the only reason I went to Jake's last night was to see Jake. I retrieved my car from the bar and parked it back home. Walking into work later that morning, I intentionally focused on other things: the cloudy day, the light it cast, the architecture, the cold. I sang songs in my head. I counted steps. This demeanor was the new me. I was being ridiculous. I'd known Jake for a few months a few years ago and we'd seen each other only a handful of times in the last month or so. These few encounters were not enough by which to be bewitched. I was done with poking around Thomas's life. Not every murder was solved; not every question must be answered. I'd stay out of it. Yep.

I got through the week without running into Pearson or hearing from police detectives. By Thursday, my resolve to stay out of it was waning. I was curious, and that curiosity did not abate. So when Thomas's landlord called early the following week to say he was clearing out the apartment and did I want the artwork, I was back in. Fuck Pearson's paranoia. Damn that I was a murder suspect. I told him I'd be over on Friday to gather it all up. He said he'd be there all day.

When I got there Friday afternoon, an ungodly frigid day—it must have been in the low twenties—there was a rental truck parked in front with the back doors open and a ramp up to a nearly empty truck. I thought it was overkill for the small amount of stuff Thomas owned, but maybe this wasn't his only load. With the truck taking all the available parking, I had to park around the corner. The double front doors were propped open. I met McAllister coming down with an armful as I was going up. He nodded and said the apartment door was open.

McAllister had heaped all the artwork against one wall. It would definitely take me a few trips loading it into the car. I was surprised to see the portfolio of Pearson still there. I thought the police would have taken it. As I started making slow, careful trips up and down the stairs, I thought about the repercussions of having the notorious collection. It felt too intimate to keep. The art was some of the best Thomas had done. I wondered if there was a way I could ask Pearson if he wanted it. There was something between them, clearly, whether Pearson would admit to it or not. Maybe I could just leave it for him, and he could decide.

On my last trip, I stood and looked around the almost empty apartment. *How fucking sad.* My eyes filled. There was a time in my life where I didn't cry at everything. I was getting sentimental in my old age. This is what I told myself, but I knew better. The books, too, had been carefully piled against a wall, the cases gone. I saw the old *Anatomy for the Artist* book and, on impulse, slid it out of the stack and tucked it under my arm. My volume of poetry was on top of another. I put it in my coat pocket. The last of the artwork was, thankfully, in portfolios, including the Pearson. With the funky holes cut in the cardboard for handles, it was easily managed. I met McAllister on the way down and let him know I was done. He nodded and continued up the stairs.

As I came around the corner to where my car was parked, I could see someone standing with the back door of my Honda open, rifling through the stack of portfolios. I'd left the doors unlocked for convenience. I yelled something scary like "Get the fuck away from my car, asshole." He turned to look at me, his face under a full balaclava and he ran the opposite way down the street. Jesus. Leave a car unlocked for five minutes.

I drove the stuff home and began the laborious process in reverse, stacking it all on my kitchen table. I'd have to make a decision on where to store it all. I thought I'd hang a few somewhere in my house, but I'd do it later when I didn't feel so raw. It was only early afternoon when I was done. I made a cup of tea, pulled Ransom's card from my wallet, and grabbed my cell phone. In my front room, I sat and dialed the number.

"Ransom" was the gravelly answer after two rings. It was noisy in the background. Phones ringing, voices. I imagined the large room where they all sat and wondered if Jake was there, across from him.

"This is Ian Start." I waited for confirmation of recognition.

"Yes, Professor Start. What can I do for you?" So formal.

"Nothing really. Well, just two things. I've, um, taken ownership of Thomas Wilson's artwork. I thought you should know that. Nobody else wanted it and, well, I did." It was more complicated, but he wasn't a psychologist. "Also, I have the portfolio of the Andrew Pearson studies. Err, I guess I'm curious why the police wouldn't want to keep them. It seems like, well, a clue, perhaps."

"Oh, I see. Well. Thanks for letting us know where Wilson's artwork is. As for those pictures, since they were discovered after the crime scene was released, they wouldn't be any use to the case. Anything discovered because of them would be dismissed because anyone could have had access to the apartment and could have put that portfolio there after the fact. You see?"

"I do. But what about fingerprints?"

"We did take a few random samples to test for fingerprints. But again, we wouldn't be able to use them in a trial." I fleetingly wondered how they had made the decisions of which to take: color, composition, lighting?

"Hmm. Can I ask how the investigation is going? I assume, or hope anyway, that I'm not your only suspect." I tried to sound conversational. I think I sounded glib. There was a pause at the other end. A long pause during which it was clear he'd put his hand over the phone and was talking to someone. It was entirely muffled, masked by the sound of a hand scraping on the receiver.

"I'm going to put you on hold for a minute, Professor Start. Will that be okay?" Exceedingly polite, definitely tense.

"Yes. Of course." Definitely confused, exceedingly curious. It was a long, long minute. Close to five of them.

When Ransom came back on the line his raspy voice sounded tired and exasperated. "Thanks for holding. Professor Start. I must apologize. You are no longer a suspect. Forensic and IT information came back a few weeks ago that definitely cleared you, though someone clearly tried to implicate you. You should have been informed of this, and I was under the impression that my partner, Detective Quinn, had. That he did not is inexcusable and will be addressed."

I sat back, shaking my head. Why would he let me walk around with this...this... What is it that we feel when accused wrongly? Moral outrage, of course, but there is a less assured undercurrent. It's not guilt, but it feels like it. My shock turned to a smoldering anger. "Thank you, detective. And would you please inform Jake that I thought the apology *you* offered on *his* behalf was lovely." I clicked off. Bastard! My hands were shaking with fury. When had he known? When he kissed me had he known? I couldn't make sense of it. I didn't want to make sense of it, actually. I was really tired of painful answers. I headed to the kitchen to warm up my tea and to add a large splash of brandy.

Chapter Ten

The rest of the weekend was a blur of just trying to stay busy. I avoided the mess of artwork in the kitchen by avoiding the kitchen. I stretched canvases. I re-primed old ones. I ate out. I went down to Rita's on Sunday morning so she wouldn't have to sit among the stacks of Thomas's drawings that I wanted to ignore. I let two phone calls from Jake go to voice mail, which he did not use. *Fuck him.* I didn't tell Rita what had happened, only that I was no longer a suspect.

Thankfully, Monday did finally come, and I could throw myself back into the deadening world of academia, trying to enjoy teaching my classes. I didn't see Pearson. Jen had no reports outside of a Pearson/Katya argument, nothing new there. There were no signs of Justin. I hadn't decided what to do with the infamous portfolio. Two things I cannot do is trash or destroy art or books. It's not in my constitution, mealy though it may be. I'd have to keep it or find it a home. I wondered if Pearson knew I had it. I should have asked Ransom while I had him on the phone. It was undoubtedly a secret for someone, living or dead. *I don't want other people's morbid secrets cluttering up my life. I've enough of my own.*

I drank. I ate. I slept. I dreamed... I dreamed Jake was taking me in his mouth, and I was getting close. That tender ache of prerelease so corporeal. I woke with a painful erection that I could only finish off with a lump of regret in my throat.

The week crept by. I still wanted to find out more about Thomas, but I'd run out of ideas. Pearson was definitely off the resource list. I wondered if some of the illustration students knew Thomas; maybe I'd ask Hanna if she'd mind asking around in her classes. Would the request be pushing boundaries? Perhaps, but I wasn't getting information anywhere else. And, for me, a question asked needed an answer. I knew now that even when I wanted to let it go, I couldn't. The police may get the murderer, but I wanted the story. Not just motive, opportunity, blah, blah, blah, but what got him there. Police don't care about such things outside of how it informs the end. I left a message on Hanna's voice mail.

Thursday, I drove to work. My leg hurt, I felt discouraged, I was lonely but didn't want to see anyone. I taught my class. Bought takeout and headed home. I was letting myself in the back door, struggling with the lock and the takeout bag. As the door swung open, I caught a glimpse of a quick movement behind me, a reflection in the window.

*

I was in a hospital. I had a vague and distant recollection of a ride. I hadn't opened my eyes due to a crushing headache, but I knew where I was. The noises, the repugnant antiseptic smell... Wait... Had I never left? My leg still the open wound?

"I can't be here," I mumbled.

A familiar voice responded, "You're safe. You're at the hospital." No. That wasn't what I meant.

The next time I woke, I ventured an open eye. The world was preternaturally bright in the center and darkly fogged at the perimeters. I ventured to open another eye. My head continued to pound, and now I was pretty sure I was going to vomit. I looked around and saw that I must be in the emergency room. I had an open view to the front desk, no doors, no walls, just curtains separating the exam areas. Standing at the counter were two people, one a man in scrubs. But my attention latched onto a pale tawny head.

Rita often teasingly admonished me that we could have more than one feeling at a time. I was having a few. "Uh, excuse me, but I'm pretty sure I'm going to be sick." The guy in scrubs hurried over and stuck a U-shaped bowl under my chin. He raised my bed, and I sat forward a little and let loose. Not much there, but my nausea abated. Jake was standing at the foot and gave a small smile. Christ, he was beautiful. I put my head back against the bed and winced at the sharp pain. Touching the knot and a line of stitches with my fingers, the whole incident came flooding back. Someone brained me. Oh. Okay. That's why Jake was here. Just doing his job.

The scrubs guy began going through his assessment. Checking reflexes, asking questions, and then had me squeeze his fingers, press with my feet. "We're going to send you up for a CAT scan to make sure there's no bleeding or swelling. If there's not, you can go home. You'll have to have someone stay with you to keep you awake for a few hours. Then to wake you up every few hours until tomorrow night." I nodded. "Okay. No alcohol, sleeping pills, ibuprofen. Aspirin is fine, or Tylenol with codeine if you want it. Just waiting for someone to come get you. You want something for nausea? Pain?" I shook my head—a huge mistake. He left.

Jake stood silently. I wasn't going to help him out. I stared at him evenly. "How are you doing?" he ventured with a tone of caution.

"Lovely, you?" As I've said, sarcasm is not the best road to communication, but I'm an expert, plus I was in pain and still angry and hurt.

Jake sighed, came around to the side of the bed. He sat on the little doctor stool, which put him too low. He stood. He looked nervous. I was glad.

"Do you remember what happened?" His voice was soft, but it might have been my funky hearing, a low hum permeating the environment.

"Yes. I got hit over the head."

Jake wiped his hand over his face, trying to keep his composure. I didn't care. Let him struggle for this.

"Did you see the person?"

"Nope. Came up from behind as I was opening the door." I shut my eyes. It was more comfortable that way for a couple of reasons, not the least of which was that Jake looked concerned, and I wanted to stay mad.

"Okay. When you're done here, I'll drive you home. There are a couple of uniforms here to take a statement, if that's okay."

"Sure, whatever." I can do petulant. I wanted to have a discussion with Jake about why he didn't tell me about my not being a suspect, but my head ached, and it literally hurt to think. "Uh, I maybe would take something for my head, Jake."

He went to get someone as I filled the uniforms in. It was a pretty short story. Before Jake got back two med assistants came to get me for the CAT scan. He was there when I got back, holding a cup of water and a smaller cup with a few pills in it. He smiled that little half smile and asked the orderlies if I was going to live. They joked around for a few minutes at my expense. Whatever. I cleared my throat and glanced at the pills Jake was holding. He got the message and handed them over. I swallowed them down and laid back. I was exhausted. I shut my eyes.

"No sleeping, Ian," said Jake.

"Just resting my head. It hurts to see."

"Okay." He patted my shoulder, and I sighed. He removed his hand. "Sorry." I shook my head. I wanted him to put it back.

"How did I get here?" I asked.

"Rita came home and saw your cat in the driveway. She found you lying in the doorway and called 911. She was here for a while. You woke up once when she was here. Do you remember?"

"Uh-uh. Maybe."

"Yeah. You may remember more later. You were in and out of consciousness the whole time. Just rest; they're checking your scan. I'm going to stay here and make sure you don't sleep, okay?" I nodded my head and felt him move a lock of hair off my forehead.

"Where'd she go?"

I could hear the smile in his voice when he said, "She went to find your fucking cat."

It was another hour before they let me go. Jake would pat me on the shoulder from time to time, his hand warm, and sometimes it seemed to linger. I could feel the hold on my outrage ebbing. By the time I was discharged, I was feeling better, able to walk carefully. I didn't have my cane and was not too stable. Jake's hand hovered behind my elbow. He was parked in front of the emergency room entrance, his police placard in the window of his black

Jeep Wrangler. He opened the passenger door for me and waited until I was in before going around to the driver's side. We hadn't spoken.

"Your place then?" he asked. I nodded. "I can stay with you tonight."

"Rita could probably stay with me. You don't have to." It seemed like the polite thing to say, but honestly, the prospect of having Jake's presence for more than a few minutes was becoming more and more agreeable. Except, I suddenly remembered this Chris fellow. I didn't want to get involved in another imbroglio. "You must need to get home anyway. It's late."

Jake looked at me, his blue eyes violet in the neon of the hospital light. "Ian, I don't need to go home. There is no one there waiting for me. There or anywhere, okay?"

I felt a little rush of adrenaline. *Must be the concussion.* I think I smiled.

*

It was only about ten minutes to my house, but like a baby, I was lulled nearly to sleep by the car. Jake shook my knee, my left knee, and I came alert with a start on a wave of trepidation. A few days ago, I was ready to face this muddle with him if he had wanted to. I'd been prepared to talk to him about my leg, about how fucked up it made me. Had that changed?

Jake noticed my flinch and asked, "Did I hurt you?"

"No. It's okay."

We were at the house. Jake pulled into the driveway and stopped behind my car. We got out, and he hurried around to make sure I didn't tip over, I assumed. The back door had been shut and locked, and as we entered, Clio was there waiting.

"Jake, help yourself to whatever. I'm going to go put sweats on and we can hang out in the front room." I trudged up the stairs to my bedroom texting Rita on the way up to let her know I was okay. She texted back to tell me Jake had been updating her all night. Huh.

I was tempted to drop onto my bed, my lovely cocoon calling. But I didn't want Jake to have to go up and down the stairs or hang around in my bedroom. That seemed too intimate. Better I crash on the sofa. I changed and headed down. Jake had a beer and was looking at some of my first editions in my antique bookcase.

As I stretched out on the sofa, Jake asked, "Why do you think someone hit you? It doesn't look like anything's missing. Did you see anything missing upstairs?"

"Shit! I meant to look." I stood up quickly, which turned out to be another mistake. I got woozy, nauseous, and the knot on my head stabbed at me. I sat back down with a plop. "Oh, fuck," I said eloquently and put my head between my legs.

"Do you need the bathroom, a bucket?"

I shook my head, which caused a shooting pain, and I groaned, but the nausea was abating, the pounding slowing. I was sweaty and uncomfortable, my head hanging like a bloodhound.

Jake came over and put his hand on my neck. Without thinking, I reached back and lay mine on top.

"I'd forgotten how beautiful your hands are," he whispered. After a few minutes, after the sweats stopped and my stomach and spinning head settled, I sat up slowly, hating to break the physical connection.

I stood up carefully, saying, "I wanted to see if that portfolio was still here."

Jake nodded and followed me to the kitchen. I pawed through the stacks, twice. Yep, it was gone. "I know it's important in all of this. I just don't know how." Suddenly I was exhausted. Thinking hurt. Seeing hurt. My head was starting to throb again. With a groan, I headed back to the sofa and dropped down, pulling my throw over me. I wanted to sleep. I was also afraid to, and not just because of the concussion. There was someone out there who did not care about life...taking a life...my life.

"No sleeping, Ian." Jake sat in the chair across from me and looked around. "No TV in this room?"

"It's in the cabinet."

"Would that hurt your head? We could find something mindless to rest your brain."

I tossed the remote for the TV to Jake. I pressed a button on a smaller remote and the TV rose from the back of a mission-style sideboard next to the fireplace.

"No regular cable, just streaming stuff. Find what you like. I'm easy. And make yourself comfortable, like feet on furniture, the table."

We settled happily on the Orson Welles, Joan Fontaine *Jane Eyre* commenting throughout on the beauty of Welles at the time, and the timbre of his baritone.

"Jake. Are there locksmiths that would come now?" I was feeling vulnerable and scared, even with Jake there. Every creak of the old house, even though familiar, I reinterpreted as sinister. Jake made a few calls, and within an hour, someone showed up to put in a new combination-type lock. He also recommended a security system and left his card. Jake handled it all.

After that, I let him choose rerun sitcoms, *Seinfeld*, the like. I'd close my eyes from time to time, and Jake would check my state of consciousness with a soft "Ian?" It was lovely. And this time, I meant it.

Morning came with a soft rosy glow, the sun filtering through sparse clouds. Jake had stayed awake the whole time. He'd said, at one point in the night, that it was part of being a detective: staying awake and not moving. I imagined him on stakeouts, sitting in a sedan with Ransom, drinking coffee, eating convenience store burritos. Sexy as hell.

He rose, saying, "You can sleep now, Ian. Do you want to stay here or go to bed?" I knew if I let him help me up the stairs, I wouldn't let him go. He needed to go; he had to go to work. He looked rumpled and tired. And I was feeling like shit.

"I'm okay here, Jake, thanks." I thought about everything he'd done for me last night and immediately got mawkish, those unbidden tears threatening *again*. "Jake. Thank you so much for watching me. It was…so, nice. Nice of you." I was sitting, looking up at his indescribably blue eyes. He bent and kissed me, a soft velvety brush of lips. My cock stirred; I was surely going to perish from want.

I got up and stood still for a moment to test my balance. It was good. I was just about to move off when Jake stepped in, grabbed the back of my neck and pressed his lips against mine. I pressed back, opening my mouth to lick at that lower lip. He parted his, and we raced into the absurd delight that is kissing. I embraced him, running one hand down his spine to his belt, knowing that going farther wasn't wise.

I am not a polite or delicate kisser. One of the things I'd always remembered about Jake was that he wasn't either. Our kisses were hot, sloppy, wet, with lots of exploration. They were about arousal. It was dirty and sexy with tongues, biting, sucking and thrusting. This kiss for me was also about life, fear for life, relief and delight at being here.

It came to a conclusion, eventually, slowly, reluctantly. "Christ," I gasped, "that was *so* good." We were still holding each other, our eyes meeting. And there in that instant I finally understood the color of those extraordinary eyes. I knew what to do now. Why had I not seen it before?

We could feel each other's cock press against the layers of fabric. Jake smiled and stepped away and unselfconsciously adjusted himself. I looked down at him doing that and shook my head with regret. I was in no shape to carry a seduction further. I sighed.

He pointed at my cell phone. "I am going to call you every two hours. You have to answer, or I'll come by." He saw me smile. "Or I'll send two of the most asshole uniforms we have to check on you."

I laughed and nodded.

"I'll come by after work, okay?"

"You should go home tonight, Jake; get some rest. Christ, you must be spent." I meant it I realized. I rather surprised myself.

"Nah, I'm coming by." He let himself out.

Chapter Eleven

I took a quick shower, careful not to wet the stitches in my scalp and crawled into bed. Jake called every two hours. The conversations were short but pleasant. Around four, when I was sounding more coherent, he asked why I thought someone would take the portfolio. It was the first time we'd broached the subject of anything relating to Thomas's murder outside of being questioned. I was still assuming the portfolio was connected, but I wasn't sure of the police's assumptions. As much as I trusted Jake, I wasn't ready to speculate with him. What if sharing led down the wrong path? And, by the wrong path, I meant back to me. I told him I didn't know. He let it drop.

By then, I was feeling better. My eyes were still a little blurry, and my head ached only slightly, but my ears still hummed. I got up, put on jeans and a long-sleeved black T-shirt. I headed down with Clio meowing at my ankles. Jake must have put down some hard food for her; there were a few kibbles left over, and she hadn't pestered me while I was sleeping. I made coffee and sat at the kitchen table looking at the disheveled mess of Thomas's work. I wondered if it was Pearson who bashed me over the head. But then, he needed to have known I had the portfolio, or suspected it anyway. I'd have to ask Jake.

I tried to consider who else would want it. Since Thomas was gone, the drawings would only be harmful to Pearson. I assume a married man wouldn't want anyone to know the drawings existed. They were a testimony to some kind of closeness. I remembered what Pearson said to me in our short exchange: "Stay away from my family." Did he think I was going to tell someone? Was he worried I'd blackmail him or something? There was more panic in his eyes than anger. I couldn't figure it out. He'd slept with scores of women, did not particularly conceal the fact, then gets involved with a man, and suddenly all hell breaks loose. I needed to stop thinking about this mess. It made my headache worse.

I thought I'd feed Jake for his trouble last night. I checked out my refrigerator—sorely lacking. Takeout felt like copping out. I carefully drove to a nice, albeit expensive, butcher shop that I go to from time to time. I chose five large lamb shanks; we could split the fifth if we wanted to. I thought I'd braise them and have a creamy polenta to go with it, some roasted Brussels sprouts, and a simple salad. I had some ice cream for dessert if he went that route. It had been a long time since I made food for a romantic interest. Huh, romantic interest... That sounded nice, though terrifying.

As I walked the block or two back to my car, my head started to pound, and I found myself jumping at every odd noise, creak of a gate, and looking around at every footstep. I felt like prey, though I had no reason to think whoever hit me would be back. They had what they'd come for. I scurried into my front seat and headed for home where I immediately swallowed a few Tylenol. Then I started straightening out the mess in the kitchen. I put on music at a low volume to keep my mind occupied. But minds go where they want, and I started thinking about Jake. I knew what I wanted to happen. I just wasn't sure how to get there. Should I clue him in thoroughly on my scar, my fear? Maybe it would be best if I let the evening go as it goes. If it falls apart, then it does. I just really did not want it to.

I was able to rest a little while the lamb slowly cooked. Jake made it over around eight, just as the lamb was done. I'd set a decent table, not too intimate, but in the dining room. We kissed as I let him in the back door, and it reminded me of the domestic pleasures I'd been missing these last few years.

"Wow, something smells good. This is a nice change from frozen dinners and canned soup." He slipped out of his sports coat, hung it on the back of a chair, undid his shoulder holster, and laid it on the kitchen table.

Dinner was quiet. I think we were both a little nervous. At one point, I'd asked about the investigation.

"There's a lot I can't talk about. People don't get that there are privacy issues in police work too. You read a mystery and the cops are telling everybody everything. We don't know the web of things, you know. Like if I told you something and it somehow made its way back to a person of interest, say, it could really mess things up, put you in danger too. And if we blabbed stuff no one would talk to cops. People have to trust us. It would be like if I were a shrink and started talking about my clients. It's not that I don't trust you, you know."

"I get it. No problem. It's funny, but I think I care less about who murdered Thomas than I do about what got him there. I feel like I let him down." I met his eyes, which were warm and unguarded.

"Well, he was living a pretty complicated life. It seems he was getting most of his money from sex work. We never found a phone, which is how he probably did a lot of his transactions, but maybe he went down to the piers on

Angel Street. Don't know if that played a part in his death. There were almost no physical clues at the scene. His computer was used, after he was shot though, to type out that email implicating you. And there" –he smiled sheepishly— "I told you more than I should have." I nodded, and we ate in companionable silence. Afterward, sitting on the sofa in front of the fire we reminisced a little, an air of sorrow tingeing the conversation. I wanted to move nearer, but fear washed over me like a hot wave from an unnatural ocean.

Jake seemed to sense my hesitancy and said, "This goes where you want it to go, Ian. No pressure."

Without thinking, I was next to him, my hand in his wiry nut-colored hair. His scruff scratched and rasped as our lips connected. Jake thrust his tongue in, and I met it with a nip and drew it in.

"Upstairs," I groaned into his mouth. Breaking the kiss, I stood and took his hand. Powerful and calloused, it closed around mine and we stumbled up to my bedroom stopping to kiss and press into each other, knocking pictures awry on our way up the stairs.

I turned to him when we entered the room, stripped off my shirt and Jake's too. His hand slid down my sides and around, coming to rest at my back, his fingers sliding below the waistband of my jeans, as mine found his ass and pulled him to me. His skin was hot, his muscles bunching and flexing against my bare chest. We kissed again, his tongue pointed and intent, exploring my lips, my teeth, my tongue. He moved away a little as his hands moved to my front. He started to unzip my jeans. I froze, and he took a step back.

"What is it?" he said.

"So, why don't you just...strip and slip under the covers. I'll meet you there." I raised a brow rakishly hoping to divert his attention. Jesus, that was not me.

Jake wasn't buying it. "What's wrong, Ian? Just tell me. It's pretty clear that this has to do with your leg. What is it?"

I felt as though I were on that abyss in my dreams. The fear brought a sticky sweat to my brow. Jake was here right now, and I didn't want to ruin that. But I knew Jake. He was never much for diversion.

"Here's the thing, and if it's too much, it's okay. I'll understand, really." Well, I'd understand, but I'd be crushed. "I got cut a few years ago. A little accident, no big deal. It was just a small cut, but it got infected. Badly infected. Flesh-eating infected, and it took some muscle too. There's a scar, a huge, long, deep scar. Jake, it's bad. Ugly. Horrible. People have walked away because of it." God. I didn't want to go on. I did not want to show him.

"Drop 'em, Ian," Jake demanded. So I did. Jeans do not fall gracefully to the ground, so I had to bend to push them down along with my boxers so he could get the full view. He wanted this show. My cock sprang up still somewhat ready to go but flagging quickly. I turned the offending side to him. Jake looked for a few seconds, raised his head, and met my eyes. Then dropped to his knees at my leg.

"God, Ian. This *is* awful; it must have been so painful." He reached up to touch the great divot in my glute with one cool finger and traced the peaks and valleys of the rift. I shivered. I hated touching it, but Jake's touch was gentle, curious.

"Horrible. That's what it is. Stuff of nightmares."

"Nah, it's you. You are not the stuff of nightmares." He began to kiss his way up along the side of my scar, starting near the bottom and ending at my ass. My knees gave way in relief, and I ended up kneeling in front of Jake on the soft rug.

"It's *my* stuff of nightmares," I whispered in the spot where his neck met his shoulder. He put his arms around me, his fingers in my hair. His tongue touched my earlobe and traveled its convoluted path to its center, and then he sucked my lobe into his mouth and bit. My dick was instantly hard again. "Jake" was all I could gasp. Then we were kissing again, hungry, wet, smacking kisses. Jake reached down and stroked us with one hand.

"What do you want, Ian?" he murmured. I wasn't sure what he was asking.

"I want you here, with me, right now, and again tomorrow, whenever you can."

"No, babe, what do you want, right now? Tell me how you want it." *Ah.*

"Fuck me, Jake... I want you to fuck me."

Jake leaned down and bit at my nipple, sucked and flicked it with his tongue, then stood suddenly. His long, thick cock bobbed in front of me, and before he could move, I grabbed his ass and took him in my mouth. He groaned long, low, and throaty, and I knew I'd want to hear that sound again. I teased the head with my tongue, running it over and around the edge, and touching the slit at the tip, tasting his salty, slightly bleachy precome. Jake grabbed my arms to haul me up and demanded, "Bed."

We lay on our sides kissing, legs entwined, hands and arms tangling in exploration. Jake's skin, gold-tinged by his fine bronze body hair, was soft, his muscles defined. His was a far more attractive body than mine. I wondered, briefly, what he felt when caressing me: skin and bones, nobs and angles... His hand fell to my ass, my defective ass, but did not hesitate in its gentle petting, falling naturally into the unnatural dips, and out again, as if it were a normal formation. He grabbed the full of it, stretching me open. I slid my bent leg up so it rested on his hip, inviting his fingers to touch my opening. "Lube?" he whispered. I twisted and reached into my bedside drawer for a condom and a few single-use lube packets I'd picked up at a health fair a few years ago. They'd been shoved far back in the drawer. Jake tore one open and smeared his fingers. He reached back, and I felt the cold dampness in my crack as his fingers sought the target.

"It's been a long time, Jake." My voice shook a little, in fear, excitement, regret. The last time I'd been entered, had been, in fact, with him. My eyes closed, I felt him nod. He slid one finger in, slowly testing the muscle. From this position he could not get far, so he slid down to a kneeling position, letting me roll partially onto my stomach with my leg still pulled up, my chest and stomach supported by pillows.

"I want to watch your face," he said quietly. He drizzled more lube on his finger and slid one back in slowly, pushing past the tension. Then another finger.

"Ah..." was the only sound I was capable of. Jake spread his fingers, gently pulled out, pushed in, and I felt the muscle give.

"There," he whispered through a smile. I looked back at him and smiled too. He turned his hand over, palm down and pressed in looking for that spot.

There is a fine line between sexual climax and pain. We all know the sweet ache of impending orgasm. As Jake drew me near, hitting and teasing that spongey, uniquely male spot, the line suddenly blurred, and I was hurled back in time bringing the past to the present in an instant and inexpressible clarity. *What is the word I need?* was my irrational thought. *Quit!* As I half yelled "No!" I shoved my body violently away from Jake's hand, up toward the top of the bed, whacking my stitched head hard on the headboard. Still, I was back there in that hospital of two years ago, with the open wound, and the pain as real and visceral as if it were that instant. I stared, not seeing outward but seeing the long past reality of it inward: my leg gutted as it was then. Inward, outward didn't matter; the pain of it, the sight of it, did.

Eventually, eons later, I heard a persistent whisper. "Ian... Ian... Ian..." and felt a gentle hand on my right leg, as still as a frightened mouse. I came back. I was sitting pressed against the bed's headboard.

"Ah, fuck" was my lame statement as I returned to the present. "Jesus, Jake, I am so sorry. That was horrible of me. I don't know what made me do that." But I did know. I shoved the heels of my hands into my eyes and rubbed. Rubbed at the humiliation, the disappointment, the surety that I would never be right again.

"What happened, Ian?" Jake's tone was even, kind, curious. "You were...gone. Where did you go?"

What was I supposed to do? Claim insanity? Explain flashbacks? Tutor rather than make love? To do anything but pull the comforter, or a slew of fucking comforters, over my head felt exhausting. But Jake deserved some kind of answer.

"I have these flashbacks." Yeah, let's keep it stupidly simple. "Jake. I wanted this. You don't know how much." I stopped, gathering my wits a little and deciding how to explain. "When I was in the hospital with my leg, all I heard from the social workers was how fucked-up I was going to be. And they were right, I am. I'm sorry, Jake." I released an involuntary sigh. "You are the most beautiful man I've ever met. I think of you all the time, and I feel like there's an ocean between my wanting you and my being able to have you." I smiled and with a little remorse added, "If I were you, I'd seriously consider getting dressed and getting the hell out." And a tiny part of me did want him to go. The lazy, complacent part. The part that didn't think that there was a whole lot for anyone to stay for.

"Did what we were doing cause a flashback?" He looked worried like he'd done something wrong.

"No. Yes. No, it's complicated. I don't always know what triggers them, but sometimes it's as plain as pain. Or remembering pain, or the potential of pain; maybe not pain but something my brain thinks is like pain, and sometimes it just happens. It's from my time in the hospital. It wasn't...good." Jake had moved up to sit next to me against the headboard. I tried to look at him; my head turned toward him, but I couldn't make my eyes meet his. Why did I ever think I would not screw up this attempt to bring some normalcy to my life?

"Well, did I hurt you? Has this happened before during sex? What should I do? What works?"

Yeah. He's assuming that I have vast experience with flashbacks *in flagrante delicto*. I was feeling more and more like a fool for even trying intimacy again. "Well, I have not been particularly sexually active since my injury, Jake, to tell you the truth." I shrugged my shoulders lamely.

"Ah." A simple expression packed with something ambiguous. I stretched my legs out, trying to relax. We adjusted our positions until we were half prone, pushing pillows around to support us. He slid his arm around my shoulders and pulled me back so I lay against his chest, my head below his chin. He kissed me on top of my head. I pulled the covers up as he wrapped his arms around me.

"Don't give up on me. I want to try this again." I was putting on a little bravado.

"Absolutely." He paused before he said, "Ian, tell me what it was like in the hospital, with your leg."

"I don't really like to talk about it." I hated talking about it. I didn't talk about it.

"Yeah, sure." He took a breath, and I knew he wasn't finished. I started to tense. He rubbed my arm as if to calm me. "I was learning to meditate a few years ago, and when I was struggling with it, my teacher told me a story. I'm not a great storyteller, but I'll try. So, there was a student that would come to his instructor every day and complain about how hard it was for him to meditate. He said that his toe hurt him, and the pain messed up his meditation. Every day the teacher would say, 'Yes, I know your toe hurts, but you have had a very difficult childhood; let's talk about that.' This went on for weeks, the student would start off about his painful toe, the teacher would ask him about his childhood. Then one day, the student came in and said 'Teacher, let me tell you something I realized about my childhood.' The teacher responded, 'Ah...let's talk about your toe.'"

"You think I should see a therapist." I had heard this suggestion from every person in my life. I forgave them for saying it. They forgave me for not going.

"I don't know, I think you should tell your story. I don't think it matters who you tell it to. I'd like it to be me, but maybe it's too soon for that."

"I think I'd come off as pathetic."

"Just because a story has pathos doesn't mean its main character is pathetic."

That resonated. I don't really believe in the road to Damascus or other revelatory myths. But what Jake said defined the difference between the story and the man living the story. I tried to make sense of my thoughts. We were quiet for a long while.

"Can you stay?" I sighed into his chest. He nodded.

Sometime in the night we woke and came together. With a languid intensity, we ground against each other, kissing, then stroking, until the release came, first for me and then him. We fell back to sleep, sticky and replete.

Chapter Twelve

Jake left midmorning with the promise he'd call later. We had lain in bed late, talking, our legs entwined. He'd asked about Arty, what had happened. It's a story I struggle in telling. I told him that he had stuck by throughout my time in the hospital, managed the lawsuit, made time to come up from Manhattan more often for a while during my recovery. But something changed. I told Jake I thought it was me. That I'd lost something of myself, not just muscle, but strength of soul, maybe. Arty had always viewed me as more "alpha" than I ever felt. I admit it was flattering; I played it, enjoyed it, lived it. After, though, I didn't have it in me to be anything but injured. I'd become a disappointment to him. He was horrified by the scar. He wouldn't look at it. Sex was infrequent, then nil. When sex happened, it was under the pall of darkness or under covers. I started to feel invisible. He began to pick fights. Not just over unimportant stuff but real issues that he refused to compromise over. He was angry with me because he wanted me to just bounce back, and in his view, I never did enough to ensure that I did. The more he pushed and urged and bitched, the more frozen and injured I became. I could see in his eyes that he just wasn't there anymore. He came up less and less, seemed to be busy when I came down. I finally let him go. He was relieved. I was...surprised. A piece of me had held on to a crumb of hope that he'd not want to go, would want to work things out, would say that nothing, not even an ugly injury, could or would affect his love for me. When he didn't, the last piece of an intact soul crumbled. When we'd sorted our belongings, Arty's filled a half a box. No clothes. Toiletries, a book or two. What I took from his place was quadruple that. "He thanked me, for Christ's sake," I told Jake. Huh. That was a little angry.

"What an asshole," said Jake.

"No. This thing happened, and it was just bigger than both of us. That's how I want to see it."

"Yeah, well, I don't." His eyes flashed with annoyance. Maybe with some spirit that I lacked. "I'd like to think I would have stuck by you, helped you find your strength again."

"Jake. This may not be the best time to ask you, but I need to know." He looked a little wary. "When you kissed me that day in my studio, did you know I wasn't a suspect anymore?"

He had the decency to look ashamed, so I knew the answer.

"I did," he said. I started to get out of bed, but he pulled me back. "Look. I had every intention of telling you at the time, started to tell you. But we got a little distracted, and then you pissed me off, and I...well, I didn't think of it until I got to my car. I was still pissed so... Fuck. This all sounds so lame." He rolled onto his back, stared up at the ceiling. "I fucked up, Ian. I'm sorry." He turned to look at me. "I'm sorry."

I believed he was sorry. It left me a little cold that he could do that, but I'd engaged with him knowing he'd done it. I'd forgiven him before last night. Was I picking at a scab again? *Move past it, Start. For a change, move along.*

*

It disturbed me when Jake had confirmed that Thomas was mired in the sex trade. I knew some students did it temporarily, with little consequence, or so they said, as a way to make money to get through school. But you'd have to be an idiot to think that it wasn't risky on a lot of levels. I wondered if one of his customers had killed him. Somebody seemed to have beat him up at some point. Did that mean the whole portfolio fiasco was unrelated? Maybe. But Pearson had been contacted by the police. He would be the only one, except the killer perhaps, who knew if there was a connection to Thomas's murder and the artwork. Something went on between the two of them, of that I was sure. Pearson's apparent homophobia was either a ruse or maybe he just hated that he could be attracted to a man. He wouldn't be the first self-loathing queer in the world. So, what would it mean if people found out about it? More than if they found out about his female lovers? Most people knew about them. Did his wife? After thirty years of his dicking around, she must. If it was men he was screwing, would that be different? Why? I always got the feeling she disliked me primarily because I was gay and out. Perhaps a gay affair would be the deal breaker. Deal. That word felt apt. The gossip, and to be fair, what I had observed, was that Marge Pearson was a genuinely unpleasant person. We'd all gossiped about what kept them together.

I was in my den, with a cup of tea, checking my email, when I got lost in those thoughts. On a whim, I searched Andrew Pearson's name. There were plenty of hits. Many were RISD oriented. I searched again, subtracting RISD. He had a current show in a gallery in Chelsea but was represented by a gallery in SoHo called Lenz NYC. He was also with a gallery in Los Angeles Arts District, of the same name, Lenz, with LA after it. His bio was pretty boilerplate, revealing nothing, using a lot of prose. Articles that mentioned him were equally uninformative, but a few indicated support from his wife. Hmm. Support can mean a lot of things in the art world, and Marge Pearson did not seem like a muse. Money maybe?

I searched Margaret Pearson with Andrew Pearson. Yes. Hits. Margaret Pearson owned a gallery in SoHo and one in LA, not surprising to me at this point, both named Lenz. Wikipedia stated that Margaret Pearson was born Margaret Thayer Weld in Boston, of what was essentially a Boston Brahmin family. The description was a puritanical yet thinly veiled hint to some impressive wealth. It was also Brahmanic in its winded description of all the Welds' philanthropic endeavors. Okay. Was Andrew Pearson a philanthropic endeavor?

Money, for a talented, but unknown, artist can be a pretty big motivator. Outside his art, Pearson was not cited in any other way. Just a regular Joe with an art degree, like most of us. I wondered about how well preserved the Puritan "morals" were in Margaret Thayer Weld Pearson. Homophobia? Any of these conjectures could affect the lengths to which Pearson would want his "unsavory" activities, and proof thereof, kept quiet. Yet he didn't even know the portfolio was out there, so to speak. Shit. I'd have to tell him. Monday.

*

Jake did call late in the day, sounding gruff, tired, harried. "Ian, we've picked up another homicide. It's going to be really hectic for the next couple of days. Its gang-related so it'll mean working nonstop."

"Oh, sounds bad. Do you want to call me when you're free? What works?"

"Yeah, I'll check in with you when I can. You can call me too. I'll talk if I can. I just don't think we'll be able to get together, probably until next weekend at least."

"Okay. No problem." There was a little awkward pause. One of those where everyone thinks they know what everyone else is thinking.

"This is not a blow off, Ian, if that's what you're thinking." Effing mind reader, eh?

"Well, that just makes me feel like a girl," I snorted.

He laughed. "No, you're not a girl. It's just early in this, well, whatever it is, and I didn't want you to, well... Look, it's happened to me, the blow off, so I didn't want you to think—"

"I might have, but not now. Thanks, Jake."

"Okay. I'll try and call tomorrow night, okay?"

"Sure, if you can."

We clicked off. Dammit! I was going to ask Jake if Pearson knew I had the portfolio. I didn't even know if he'd been questioned about my assault. I couldn't think of who else would have an interest in it, but I couldn't see Pearson hitting me. I think if he knew I had it, he'd just ask me for it. No, there was something more sinister here, and I wanted an answer.

Jake called around ten while I was lounging on the sofa watching television. He said he was sitting in a car on a stakeout and "bored to tears." I took the opportunity to ask him about the portfolio.

"I called him about his whereabouts Thursday night. He was out of Providence in New York from Thursday afternoon on until Friday afternoon. It checks out. I didn't mention the portfolio. Why?"

"Well, I think he should know the thing is out there. It could be detrimental to his private life, you know? I'm going to let him know Monday."

"Ian, don't mess around in this. I can tell him. It's probably better that it comes from the police."

"I want to tell him. I took ownership of it. I was responsible for it." I also wanted to see his reaction, but I didn't share that aspect.

We talked about what I was watching on TV: *Luke Cage.* He snorted and teased me about watching hunky men shows. The conversation went to current TV preferences. It was nice, an easy going, get to know each other again exchange. He lamented the boredom of stakeouts. He was hoping the guy they were watching would lead them to the murder suspect. I asked if it was dangerous. He said less for him than the SWAT team or uniforms that would go in first if they found the suspect. I wondered aloud if I'd ever asked him about the danger of his job back when he was in Brockton and we were seeing each other. I realized we had been together for months back then, but I knew so little about him. Had I even bothered to worry about him?

"We didn't do a lot of talking," said Jake. We laughed a little at that. It was true. We spent time together, had a lot of sex, went to museums, movies, dinners, but didn't delve very deeply into each other's lives. I think, at the time, I resisted knowing him too well.

We disconnected after a bit. I reflected on how nice it was to have someone call to chat, to see how I'm doing, someone to make my heart lift and beat a different rhythm.

*

Monday was a gray day. It was cold, and the wind was steady off the ocean, the damp seeping through winter coats and making people irritable. But the smell of the sea has always enraptured me. The briny scent of marine creatures, vaguely fishy, vaguely smelling of clams from the seagulls who'd drop their armored catch on empty parking lots to crack them open, feasting on the fat innards and leaving shards of white and purple quahog shells spattering the expanse. It is primal, my attachment to the ocean; it is from whence we come, and I feel a natal connection to it. Salt is everywhere in our bodies. We taste our tears, our juices, our blood...salt.

Sunday morning, I'd cautiously updated Rita on my fiasco with Jake. She seemed unperturbed by the flashback, which was reassuring. "Don't let history dictate your future, Ian. Just because it happened, doesn't mean it'll happen again. You know the drill: breathe deep. Relax."

Jen was not at the desk when I got to school on Monday. It was the new student assistant, one of the three or four that staffed the reception desk throughout the year. I couldn't remember his name. Austin...Angus...? I chatted with him for a few minutes, asked him how he liked working in this department. Did he get along with the teachers?

"Artists are temperamental, you know?" I joked.

"Yeah, everyone's pretty cool, except Professor Pearson. He seems a little...intense."

"Oh? Has he come down too hard on you? He can be difficult." I wanted him to keep talking about Pearson. Curiosity? Empathy? Oh, hell no, I was looking for info.

"Not me. But he was yelling at that Katya the other day. Didn't seem too cool to me, but what do I know?"

"Huh. What were they arguing about, do you know?"

"All I heard was Katya calling him a piker, and he said he wasn't her sugar daddy." Augie/Aaron snorted a laugh. "I know what sugar daddy is, so I guess piker means a cheapskate."

"Hmmm. I know they argue. Is that a common theme, do you know?" Their tiff was piquing my interest.

"Jen says she's always after him for money, nicer dinners, gifts." He shrugged. "I thought teachers weren't supposed to fu...um, fraternize with their students."

"Well, some schools have policies, some don't." I didn't want to get into a morals discussion.

After class, I headed to meet Jake at Harry's for a beer and maybe a few sliders. It was crowded with students. I like being among the young. Their energy and, these days, political outrage always gives me hope. I waited for a table. I was a little early, and Jake showed up just after I'd found one. Jake got an O'Doul's. He thought he may have to go back to work. I chose an Irish cider. We got a mix of sliders and fries to share. He chatted about how his gang case was going, lamenting not having much involvement as there was a special unit for gang-related crimes. I asked him about how many homicides he'd have going at any given time.

"Two or three, depending on how many there are. Rarely one. You're thinking about how much time we're spending on Thomas, right?" He cocked his head at me. God, I loved that.

"I guess. I feel a little at sea. There are things I want to know, am curious about, but I don't want to screw things up for you. Do family and friends of loved ones do that a lot? Get in the way?"

"Oh, sure. It can be annoying. Sometimes, like with gangs, it's fucking dangerous. But we're supposed to be understanding. Henry's better at it than I am. I can go off on people. That can backfire." He related a story about when he pissed a father off, and the father went out and found the guy who had stabbed his daughter to death. The father himself was killed in the process. "That was bad. Took me a long time to get past it." He looked down at his plate for a moment and then shook his head, trying to toss off the memory. Obviously changing the subject, he brightened and asked me about how teaching was going, whether I was still as into it as I had been. I paused as I thought about that question. The 'had been' threw me, but I realized he was talking about when we were seeing each other, not about the injury. But that's how I view the past now: pre or post infection. I took a few deep breaths, relaxed.

"It was terrific until the injury. The recuperation period was just hell. It still is sometimes. I didn't go back to teaching creative writing. I needed time to heal, and RISD wanted to hire me part-time. I think I changed after that, Jake, after I got sick." I stopped, not knowing where to go from there. I stared at the remnants of our meal. Persevere, says Rita. And Jake was waiting patiently, his extraordinary eyes a raft. "It's grief, I'm told. I say the recuperation was hell, but there are worse places than hell. For weeks I was forced to watch my leg...dissolve before my eyes, and there was nothing I could do. I begged them to take my leg off. Arty begged them not to. My mother couldn't stand the sight or smell of it and flew the coop. I was so sick, so lonely. Fredrick was there though. He saved me." I stopped again. That was more than I'd told anyone. Ever. How did it feel? How was it supposed to feel? I thought I was supposed to feel better. I didn't. What the fuck?

"Now what's it like for you?" He leaned forward, chin in hand, an elbow on the table.

I shrugged. "Sadder."

He reached toward me to push a lock of hair back from my forehead. "What can I do?" he asked evenly, as if there was an answer.

Jake's cell phone rang a few seconds later ending that very nice moment, and after a brief conversation, he said he had to go. I told him I was going to stay to finish my cider. He stood, paused a moment, then leaned down to kiss me. Huh. Public displays of affection are fine with me—they just have not happened much, particularly outside of gay venues or NYC. Arty and I had held hands a lot, but not kissed. I never thought much about it. Now I did. Jake's kiss went straight to my groin. I could deal with this.

I watched him walk away, a confident stride across the tile, the crease of his trousers falling straight from the curve of his perfect ass. Not a bubble butt, a high, tight, hard-as-a-rock butt. That was where my attention was as I saw him, his ass, stop and turn—but not toward me. Coming in as he was going out were Katya and a friend. Jake was definitely looking at Katya. *Well*, I told myself, *she is beautiful*. Gay, straight, or dead, anyone would take notice.

The women sat at an empty table on the other side of the room, Katya facing me. As I was finishing my cider, I looked down my glass to see her eyeing me. The table, still with two settings, and then me again. I thought little of it. Students were curious about their professors. Professors were sometimes curious about their students. I left cash enough for the bill and tip and walked out. It was only four, yet the sun was already invisible, just casting its last desperate imprint. I headed home. I had thought of going back to the office and talking to Pearson but rationalized my way out of it. *Chicken shit.*

I was ready for spring. The cold seemed to sap the strength out of my leg. Not a lot of muscle to warm up, I supposed.

Chapter Thirteen

Tuesday seemed to move like molasses. I only had one class, but all studio art classes are three-hour sessions. The model was late, so I scrambled with a still-life setup to fill the time. She came but had a bad cold and suffered fits of coughing throughout the session. I wanted to laugh; the students were pretentiously outraged at the audacity of someone actually sneezing while they were trying to draw and were making snide comments, asking her to please not cough. I tolerated it for a while until I reminded the little twits that some people had to make a living, and models didn't get sick pay. They shrugged and did a better job of muttering under their breaths. Ah, to be young and arrogant.

Normally I would have headed home after class, but I'd already put off the Pearson portfolio discussion a day. I needed to get it behind me. I headed over to the office where Jen was sitting looking at the most elaborate 3D fingernail I'd ever seen, molded into what: buildings? She would soon have the strongest individual fingers in Rhode Island by just lifting them. When I could tear my attention away, I asked what was new. I was wondering about Justin but didn't want to upset her. Those nails could probably do some pretty desperate damage.

"Nothing new under the missing sun." She chuckled at her joke.

"How much does something like that cost?" Nodding at her nail. I was, frankly, fascinated by the technology and craft behind the behemoths.

Jen snorted at me, "You don't wanna know."

I asked her if she would save it for me if one fell off. She wadded paper up and threw it at me in response. I was laughing and picking it up when Pearson came in. He headed toward his office. I had to stand and turn awkwardly, sort of hop-hop-hopping around.

"Andrew, a moment?" I puffed out.

"No time, Start," he barked as he started to shut the door. I stuck my cane in, which worked so handily I almost wanted to give it a name: Rocky, Bruiser?

"Only a minute, Pearson. It's important." He sighed and opened the door. He knew he didn't have much choice, too many witnesses for a scene. I shut the door behind me.

"Andrew, I have to tell you something that's probably going to piss you off, but if you lay one hand on me, I will clean your clock. Got it?"

He looked at me in shock and bewilderment. Like he'd forgotten his grabbing hands a few weeks ago. I looked again and wondered if he did, indeed, forget. Anyway, he nodded and sat in his desk chair.

"Look, after Thomas was killed, I went to his apartment to see what was there of his artwork. I only did it because no family or friends stepped up to claim it, and that seemed such a sad thing. I was poking around when I came across his portfolio. I didn't take it then because it was clearly hidden, and I knew the police hadn't seen it. Yes. you were right. It was me who called them. No harm intended. I just knew I'd found something they hadn't." I took a breath. I looked at Pearson, who was watching me warily, like he knew it was going to get worse, but he said nothing, waiting for me to go on.

"So, they did whatever they do," I continued. "I don't know. Later, when the landlord was clearing out Thomas's apartment, he called me to ask if I wanted his artwork. I said yes. When I went to get the stuff, the portfolio was there. I took it with me."

At that point, Pearson sat forward and said, "*You* have it!" There was some accusation behind it, but also some relief.

"Uh, so, I was letting myself in the house last week when someone knocked me out and took it." I prepared, mentally, for a tirade. Waited for it.

Andrew Pearson's eyes were that uncomfortable shade of gray that sometimes looks as though one has no irises—they are so like colorless glass. I felt like I was looking through them to nothingness. "I see," he said evenly. But his face was flushed, and his eyes flitted about in their sockets. After a very long pause, he looked at me and added, "Well. Okay, whatever."

I am not often far off in my predictions of human reactions, but his was just so at the other end of the spectrum of what I was expecting that I was stunned. I mumbled, "Okay, thought you should know" and scooted out. Did I feel like I dodged a bullet, or caught one between my teeth? I muttered a quick goodbye to Jen, who was looking at me suspiciously, and hurried out. Pearson's reaction was so surprising I started for home in a kind of daze, thinking about the implications. Were there? Maybe he didn't really care, but I didn't really believe that.

The night was cloudy, and the reflected city lights of Providence cast an unnatural but beautiful glow, so when

I stepped out of the closer, more defined orb of the streetlamps the strange ambient light seemed to say "no matter."

*

The rest of the week was unusually uneventful. I heard from Jake sporadically. I called him once or twice but seemed to only call at bad times, so I left phone calls mostly up to him. Aside from classes, I struggled to do anything productive. I felt lethargic and restless at the same time. Finding myself pouring booze earlier and earlier each day, I vowed to lay off for a while. I considered taking up pipe smoking, but Clio would probably never talk to me again. She barely put up with cologne. Maybe I should join a gym. I wouldn't mind swimming, but that would mean wearing trunks. I could get longish ones, I supposed. In the end, I watched a little television and read, then worked on another nude until late into the nights. I thought that starting a relationship with a nice man would make me happier. I'm not sure I was. But maybe I was less numb; maybe that's what my restlessness was: awakening.

Friday afternoon, Jake called. He was so excited he could hardly get words out coherently. Their diligence in tracking their suspect paid off in more than one way: they got the killer and took some heroin and fentanyl off the street. He played a significant enough role in the operation to be proud of his being part of the team. He wanted to celebrate. His exuberance was infectious, so I asked what he wanted to do. He thought for a moment and said, "Get out of Providence for the evening. I don't care where. Newport, Boston, whatever." I couldn't blame him. I supposed when you are exposed to the underbelly of a city on a daily basis, even the finer points start to look bleak.

"I'll make reservations somewhere for a late dinner, okay?" He agreed to meet here, and I'd drive. I puttered around the house trying to think of a worthy place within reasonable driving distance. I was thinking Boston when I remembered having lunch in Newport once and walking by Bouchard's Restaurant. It had an inn attached to it, too, I remembered. French, quaint, perfect. I reserved dinner for two at nine and then, on impulse, booked a room. Finding a vacancy would only have been possible in the winter, as Newport is absolutely beyond capacity with tourists in the summer. I texted Jake to tell him to be here by eight.

The night was clear. As we drove out of the Providence metro area, we started to see more stars. The moon was a little crescent, and I was reminded of my childhood, holding my thumb up to the moon to create a longer fingernail. I told Jake about the memory. He tilted his head at me and asked, "Was that to make your nail seem more feminine? I guess I'm asking about how it was for you being a gay kid. How did you make sense of it? Of the confusion?"

"Mmm. Yeah. I know a lot of my gay friends have talked about wanting to play with the girls, being more interested in 'girlish' things: hair, dress, all of that. For me, it was that I was more comfortable with girls, but I didn't *play* much. Not with other kids anyway. I was so shy. There were a few boys, the nerdier ones, who I could hang out with and not be uncomfortable. Then, when I was older, I *wanted* to hang with them." Jake chuckled. "My dad was not athletic, luckily, so there wasn't a lot of pressure to do sports things. I just sort of knew. There were no 'aha' moments. I remember just growing into it. Not that it was easy, you know that. There are so many signals that there was something different about me from very early on. All the girl-boy messages; TV, reading, Dick and Jane, the whole world, right? We're all stuck with a little shame from those messages, I think. It was a bigger shame when I was younger. I did make an announcement when I was, oh, seventeen, I guess. But no one was surprised. Everyone knew. I'd just heard so many stories about 'coming out' to the family that I thought it was something I was supposed to do. The fingernail thing was just that if you move it a certain way it fits, always. I liked that, like matching puzzle pieces. Counting on finding a way to fit them together, hoping that you will, fear that you won't. Art is like that."

"Police work is like that. That seems obvious, but I don't see how art is like that. It seems much more, spontaneous, maybe. More intuitive. But now that I hear myself say that I realize detective work is often intuitive. I always thought of art as more emotion-based, not fact-based."

"Hmm. Maybe. But art is a big world. Think of the classicists, neo classism. Very intentionally thought-out, planned, scientific even. It's all problem-solving, the difference is the problem you're trying to solve. Maybe it's more truth based. Truth being different than fact. But doesn't detective work deal in truths too? One person's truth is different from the next; you guys have to see different truths, yes?"

"Yeah, sure. We start with some facts. Examine the truths. Back up the right truth with the facts."

"The *right* truth." I was teasing a little. Jake got it and laughed.

"Okay, maybe we're getting a little esoteric, here, especially regarding police work. Let's leave the voodoo to you *artistes*." We chuckled. I poked him. He took my free hand and held it on his thigh.

We drove in companionable silence until we got to Newport.

*

The restaurant was quiet, only a few patrons. We chose a bottle of a mid-priced Bordeaux and a couple of appetizers—the house pate and the salmon tartare. I asked Jake about his experience growing up gay in South Boston.

"Well, kinda different from yours," he said with a wry grin, "You know, big Catholic family and all. Hell played a big part in all of our lives, like, all the time. That's how my mom maintained control—shame and the threat of hell. I don't remember them saying they hated gays, but my mother was church all the way. They just didn't have space or time for anyone who didn't march along in a way they understood, the way the church understood. Impatience was what I remember most. They were impatient for me to grow out of a stage. Impatient with me for just 'thinking' I was gay; after all, I liked sports, played baseball. When I reached adolescence and started to look at team members in a certain way, my dad noticed. He was pretty well read, so at first what he was thinking was that this was some sort of British boarding school-like thing, and he'd bug me to get over it, date a girl. He ignored the reality for as long as he could. Then he pretty much outed me. Not in a very nice way. He said if I was going to do this—be gay, I guess—I'd better not get picked up for doing something disgusting in a back alley, otherwise his fellow cops would find out. Old-school thinking, you know. He wasn't around a lot anyway. If he wasn't at the station, he was at the bar, so..."

The waiter came for our order. Jake chose the duck breast with a coffee crust, and I got the Dover sole with a sorrel sauce. Jake indulged me in my preference for having salad at the end.

"How did your mother react?"

Jake sighed. "You know, the thing is, through all of the hard stuff, I never ever doubted she loved me. I never thought she'd kick me out. I knew when she found out she'd be devastated, worried for my soul, but she would never abandon me. She never said it was disgusting, but there was the shame of sinfulness. She thought it was immoral, like cheaters, liars, robbers, adulterers, fornicators. She just thought I'd go to hell with the rest of the sinners. Kind of black-and-white thinking. She cried a lot. My mom was forever trying to set me up with her friends' daughters, pressuring me to date, even after I came out. Her biggest worry was who would take care of me as an adult. No wife, no care. Getting a little frantic about it all. It was hard living that lie. I knew when I was eight that I liked boys. I didn't fight it as much as hide it. But there was a lot of shame." Jake looked out toward the bay. He looked back at me with those eyes, a little sad. "Do you ever wish you weren't gay?"

Oh, what a sad, sad question. I wasn't sure how to answer. I knew where I stood; never once did I wish otherwise. "I think the closest I've ever gotten to wishing that is that I wish it wasn't so hard."

Jake nodded. He drew in a breath. "My wish is that it didn't hurt people. I hurt my mother; I'd give anything not to have." He offered up a weak smile.

"You Irish boys and your mothers." Jake chuckled. "*Mon chou.*" I laid the accent on thick; this was a French restaurant after all. "People do have some choices about what they'll be hurt over." I paused a moment, thinking about how I'd be as a father. "Sometimes it's a relief that I'll never be a parent. It requires so much...flexibility, I think."

Jake put down his wine glass, with his head cocked to the side as if he was about to say something, when the waiter brought our food and we dug in. We moaned with delight, tasted each other's food, joked about calories; he'd chosen the fatty duck, I the lean sole. I told him weight was not an issue for him; he was the most gorgeous man I knew. He blushed, told me he wished he had my physical grace, and he thought I moved like a dancer, and my hair— was so soft, a beautiful open curl—and he complained about his wiry mop. God, God, it was all so enticing. I did not want to fuck this little rendezvous up like the last time. I still hadn't told him about the room. We finished dinner, paid up, and were having a cup of coffee when I broached it.

"Jake, I hope this wasn't too arrogant of me, but if you want to stay the night here, I reserved a room. If not, that's fine. I just thought...you know...if you didn't have to work tomorrow... I mean... I don't...obviously...but I don't know your sched—"

Jake stood suddenly, startling me. "For chrissake, Start, shut up." He grabbed my arm and we headed for the reservation desk. As I checked in, I sent Jake to the bar for two cognacs. The room, on the second floor, was a deep terra cotta, almost a brick red; the furnishings were sleek, not overly feminine; black and gray were the offsetting tones, the wood of the furniture light. I liked it—very attractive—but it was the handsome man standing in front of me removing his tie that had my attention. I followed suit, undoing the top few buttons of my shirt. There was a Bluetooth music cube on the bureau, and I linked my phone, then chose some nice old classics I had stored. Johnny Hartman's lush baritone came on singing "Wee Small Hours," and I stepped toward Jake, put my arm around his waist, and took his hand. He stepped in, and we danced, if that's what you'd call it. At some point, I put my nose and lips to the crook of his neck, inhaling his spicy scent. I'd remembered the fragrance from what seemed like eons ago—in a shabby, hot little apartment in East Providence.

We didn't talk, focused on our bodies, caressing, listening to each other's heartbeat, feeling our pulse, fast and syncopated. Jake shuffled us to one lamp, shut it off, and guided us to the bed, and as we moved together, we undressed each other—kissed. Jake's head may be covered by a wiry thatch, but his body hair was soft, scant, and sparkled in the dim light. The golden path to his groin ended in tight little curls. He was toned, but not overly, he didn't maintain overly developed six-pack abs, but there was no extra padding, and the V leading down from his hips was well-defined and beckoning. I ran a finger along one side of it, and he shivered.

Not for the first time, I wondered about how I was seen through his eyes. I always felt all knees and elbows in comparison. Our hands smoothed over the planes of each other's torso, learning, memorizing. Our cocks, touching at times, twitched when we hit on pleasure points. I pulled away a little, just to stand and caress him to watch him twitch and quiver. Our eyes met simultaneously, and we kissed more urgently. He sucked my bottom lip and nipped a little. I could hear myself pant slow needy breaths. I pushed Jake back onto the bed, leaned over him and moved down, kissing, tasting, stopping at his nipple to play it with my tongue, and then I sucked hard. He groaned and I thought I'd orgasm from the sound itself. I licked and nipped my way to his cock and took him deep. He started a stream of lewd oaths: expressions of need, plans of actions, eager and primitive. I swung his legs up and around onto the bed. Kneeling between his legs I stroked him, cupped and kneaded his balls. His eyes, swollen with lust, gazed into mine, and for the first time in years, I felt desired.

"Lube?" he gasped. I leaned over the bed to my trousers and dug in the pocket for the small tubes and condoms I'd stashed. He smiled. "Good man."

Two fingers were quickly drenched and at his opening. He looked at me, huffing slightly, waiting. I watched his face as I slid one, and then two fingers in, waiting for the muscles to concede. Jake's prominent red perineum tightened with his balls; he sighed with a breathy, "Ohh." I stroked back and forth gently, the lube warming. When I pressed in to find the spongy gland, Jake restarted his filthy litany. I loved it; I couldn't get any harder, hotter. I asked him if he was ready. I think he said, "Gah." He pulled his legs farther back. I slapped the condom on and, in milliseconds, was at his entrance.

"Jake," I whispered, "Jake." And I pressed in.

It had been a long time. I knew I wouldn't last. Between the alcohol and how electric Jake felt...well, I'd try to make a good show. We found a rhythm, and I matched my stroke of his cock. Our grunts and moans filled the space, the slapping of our meeting like a metronome. I loved watching his face, his eyes closing, then opening looking straight at me while muttering profanities. "Harder, Ian, fuck me harder."

"Christ, I'll come. I'm close."

"Just do it; hit me hard."

So I did, and three strokes later, the sweet clench came, and I let go. Jake took over stroking himself as I orgasmed, and he came while I was still thrusting in the aftershock. I fell on him as I slid out, his sticky show smeared between us. I nuzzled my face into the crook that was becoming my favorite hideaway, spicy and exotic. I suddenly felt shy, realizing that this whole evening probably meant an ocean more to me than him. Jake was so...healthy. Not just physically, but emotionally. I believed this; I felt it. I rolled quickly over, grabbed a few tissues, wrapped the condom in them and tossed them in the bin. Jake reached over to stroke my back.

"That was, just...fucking fantastic." He sounded sincere.

I stood and headed for the bathroom to dampen a couple of washcloths for us. I tossed one to him. As I stood there admiring Jake, it hit me that I had not thought of my leg in any way but obliquely, distantly. And I was, at that moment, standing naked before this man, unashamed. I shook my head in...confusion? Awe?

"What? It was, Ian. You were." He looked at me, down my body, back to my eyes. "You're a cheetah, so long and lean. Beautiful." Rita once told me, after rejecting another compliment, that I should just let them wash, and she'd swept her hands from her head down, like a ballerina. So, I let it wash. I smiled, leaned over, and kissed him.

"Thanks, Jake."

Chapter Fourteen

It was the dog again.

We'd crawled under the covers spending some time petting and kissing in the dark, no words. Slowly we stilled and I rolled over, pulling Jake up behind me. It was two or so before we finally slept.

The same scenario: the dark, the muddled malachite and lapis undergrowth, the same cliff. The dog is growling and tearing at something. Christ, not my leg, I think in terror. I start to stretch to look over without getting too close and I see that it isn't my leg. It's someone else's, and I don't want to know any more, overwhelming dread weighs me and I consider stepping back, ending this life, stepping out. But a voice I know: "Ian, Ian..." desperate, in pain. His leg is in the dog's maw, and it is pulling him away. I'm frozen. I can't move forward, backward. I reach for him, despairing.

I choked awake on a "Jake!" not fully uttered.

I froze, not wanting to wake him. He stirred and muttered something in his sleep and, with a little snore, stilled. I waited a few minutes and then rose and headed to the bathroom. I closed the door before turning the light on. Looking at myself in the mirror, I could see the sheen of a fine layer of sweat covering my face, my chest. I splashed myself with cold water, drank a glassful, peed, and stood at the sink until my heart settled. I knew that going forward with Jake would mean to risk losing him and that the loss would be so much more extreme than a leg. I shut the light and slid back into bed, his warmth enveloping me immediately. I fell back to sleep thinking, *I am in over my head.*

*

In the morning, we showered together, which consisted of a lot of soap, ass grabbing, and kissing, our cocks up and ready, handily tended to. There was laughing and teasing. Had Arty and I ever laughed during sex? It felt new. We dressed and headed back to Providence after picking up takeout coffees. Jake said he was supposed to go in to work in the afternoon for a wrapup on his solved case. I wanted to ask him about Thomas's case. It felt as though he'd been forgotten, abandoned. But I also knew Jake was loathe to talk about it to me; he'd said there was a conflict. I didn't see it that way, but it wasn't my call. Still.

"So. What are you going to be working on now? Have cases lined up?" *Subtle, right?*

Jake gave me a patient look, a slight smirk. "Just ask, Ian."

That annoyed me a little, I must admit. "Why do I have to ask? Can't you offer up a little bit of information every once in a while just to let me know he's not forgotten?" I tried not to sound snippy, kept my voice neutral. I didn't know the rules here. Maybe, under the circumstances, neither did Jake.

Turning to me, with his frank and open face, he stated, "He's not forgotten, Ian." He looked back out the window, rubbing his hand over his face. "None of our victims are forgotten."

I sighed. "Well, maybe forgotten was the wrong word. But let me ask you something." I didn't wait. "If your boss, what, a sergeant?" Again, I didn't wait. "If he said, 'I want you to concentrate on X murder over Y murder, you'd have to do that, right?" Jake looked at me long enough for me to know I'd hit on something. "So, gang murders go to the top of the list, and the murder of some gay kid who tricked shuffles down to the bottom. Public interest I suppose," I finished with a snort.

"You're partly right, Ian. We are told what to concentrate on, but we're not followed around to make sure we are doing that to the letter. We follow leads when they come, as they come. Jesus Christ, Ian. You think I don't want to know who killed this kid?" He was angry, and it made me feel better to see some outrage. "We can't just go out and arrest someone either. We have to build a case, have enough evidence. Even if we know who did it, it takes time to gather everything we need."

"Okay, okay, sorry. Can you tell me anything?"

"Well, we have theories, no proof. We have 'people of interest,' no strong suspects. Whoever did the murder left nothing behind except the gun. And that's bad. It's nice to find a weapon that leads to the killer, but how often does *that* happen? The weapon was untraceable. No prints. It looks like Thomas let whoever it was in, knew him. He must have been wearing gloves. Everything we have is anywhere from circumstantial to guesswork." He sounded defeated and frustrated. "It was so simple in architecture. Someone came in. Shot him. Carefully typed the email to your dean but did not send it. That's weird, right? Who would implicate you? There's a connection there. Then he slid that other letter into Thomas's portfolio. But that could have happened earlier. This is a really tough case, Ian. But we're working it. It's very active. We do have some leads." He was looking straight ahead at the highway, a little frown creasing his forehead.

"What about when you asked me if I'd known about him getting beat up? What was that about?"

"We had a report on him from a few years ago. Someone called on a disturbance. When the uniforms got there, Thomas had been beaten pretty badly. He wouldn't identify the perpetrator or file charges, said it was a misunderstanding. The report speculated that it was a customer."

"Christ. He was prostituting. Maybe he *was* killed by a customer. I wish he'd talked to me." My frustration peaked again, and I knew I'd have to find answers. I could tell Jake wanted to. But it seemed clear to me there were more important cases to be solved than this one. I didn't say anything more.

Out of the corner of my eye, I could see Jake looking at me. He waited a long moment and then said, with some force. "Ian. I know you are curious about what happened to Thomas, that you think you failed him. You didn't. But more importantly, please, please do not poke around. We just don't know who or what you might be poking at. It could be dangerous for you. You've already been assaulted. You need to be careful here. You need to stay out of it." He sighed dramatically.

"Okay," I stated simply.

"Okay, what?"

"Okay, I'll be careful."

"Shit," Jake said with a snort.

The conversation stayed light after that. Traffic was thick, so it took over an hour to get home. I pulled up to my space at the top of the drive, and we got out. Jake stood at the side of the car as I came around.

"Want to come in for a proper breakfast? Cup of coffee?" Now that we were home, I was feeling shy, socially graceless.

"Nah, I gotta get home and get ready for this afternoon. Thanks though." Jake seemed a little reserved too. This bashfulness was silly. I stepped in and trapped him against my car, one hand on the edge of the top. I breathed, my mouth just to the side of his, rubbed my cheek against his scruff of whiskers. I loved this, this wholly male sensation, the shared sharp prick and scrape, the soft sound it made.

"Last night was incredible," I murmured into his ear. "Thanks, Jake." I moved my head up and down. Jake reached up and scratched behind my ear.

"So feline," he said through a chuckle.

We kissed. A few short pecks progressed until we were both hard. I stood back.

"Go home before you can't," I said. Jake said he'd call later and headed to his car. I watched him walk, admiring his assured gait. He moved with such intent. He gave a little wave as he backed out, and like that, I was alone.

Clio was pissed. She let me know it. Hah! One is reminded that one is not alone with a Siamese. I fed the vocalist her favorite wet food that I hated because it gave her the worst breath. I changed into jeans and a T-shirt with an old flannel shirt on top and headed to my studio. I sat looking at the canvas and felt entirely unmotivated. I started pawing through old sketches and paintings. I set aside some canvases that were not successful and not heavily textured to re-gesso and use again. Some I set aside to try to sell. Many I thought would never sell, but that I liked, I set in another stack.

I'd stashed Thomas's drawings and other artwork on a table in an unused corner. I started to casually look through them. For something to do, I began to separate the drawings from the illustrations, the canvases I'd already set to the side. Somewhere in his schooling, he'd taken a photography course, probably from Pearson, and there were quite a few 8x10s crammed into a few large yellow envelopes among the stack of illustrations. I hadn't seen these when I was at his apartment, I admit I was more interested in his drawings and paintings, but I grabbed the envelopes and headed to my comfortable leather chair to look at them.

Some were typical photography-assignment-type photos. The compositions were decent, the darkroom work okay. All of them were of the environment, architecture, nature, urban scenes. That was, until I got to the end. In the last envelope were portraits and casual shots of a young man. No one I knew, but I recognized him from somewhere. I continued to thumb through the pictures. The portrait shots were dark, moody, beautiful. He had a heavy brow bone with thick, black brows over almond-shaped eyes. His nose was long and classically Greek. His face tapered to a squared-off jaw and was punctuated with a dimpled chin. His lips were luscious; the top bowed, angling straight to the corners. His lower lip full and just a little pouty, the width as wide as the outer corner of his eyes. His hair was longish and dark, curly in a way that formed a crown. There was an almost studied intimacy in the way he looked into the camera. The other pictures were more spontaneous, playful; one was of this boy walking away from the camera, turning his head to flip the photographer off, a smirk on his face, the curls around his head faintly backlit, creating a halo. In another, the boy ran toward the camera laughing. All were in black and white. I came across one of him sprawled asleep on his stomach, the sheets rumpled around him. He was wearing dark briefs, slung low around his hips. He was neither fat nor slim. A medium, healthy, muscular build. I looked at the back of each photo. Only one had a marking: Stas. A place? A photography abbreviation? And where had I seen this face before?

I went back through Thomas's artwork. There were many life drawings that I remembered from some of my classes. And, of course, there were some I didn't recognize, probably from a different instructor's course. There were a few charcoal portrait drawings, none of the boy. I was glad to see that Thomas had a friend, though, if that's what he was. I wondered if I could find him, talk to him. Could he tell me something about Thomas, even if it was only "I was his friend"? I picked a head-on portrait out of the bunch and took it downstairs. I put it on the table in the foyer with my gloves to take into school with me on Monday. Maybe someone would recognize him.

Jake called around nine. He was definitely a little drunk, and I could hear that he was at a bar. "We're just having a little celebration, y'know?" He slurred celebration a little. "But I wanted to call before I get too shit-faced."

I laughed, told him to go have a good time, that he deserved it, and I was proud of him. And when I said that I felt a tug of, what? Not ownership, not yet partnership, no, not patriarchal pride, but what? What was that tug? Connection, perhaps. I liked it.

After we clicked off, I called Rita to see if she wanted to come up for a nightcap. She declined. I think she had someone there. I looked out the windows but didn't see a strange car, though people do walk and use other means of transportation. So, I guessed I would just give the day over and head up to bed, Clio at my heels.

Sunday was pouring rain, but Rita was at my back door, nevertheless, bearing pastries under her lime-green umbrella. We mumbled appreciative noises over the flakey heaven and slurped hot chocolate. I asked her who her company was last night.

"Mm. What company? Did I have company?" she asked with an amazingly straight face.

"Me thinkst thou didst, my dear."

She laughed and tried to say that it was just an old friend. "But *you* were gone all Friday night, and Jake's car was here." She raised her eyebrows in expectation. She is a master at deflection.

"He wanted to celebrate something, so we went to dinner in Newport and stayed over. It was nice." End of story.

"'It was nice.' Pfft. What was nice? Dinner?"

"No...yes, dinner was nice. The night was nice. The sex was amazing. So, yeah. Nice." I looked at her and quirked a smile. She returned an unguarded grin.

*

Monday was still gray, but not raining, so I walked in. I'd tucked the picture of Thomas's mystery friend into the large pocket on the inside of my overcoat. I spent the walk thinking of who I might ask about it. I'd start with Jen; she seemed to know a lot about the younger gay community. It struck me as odd that I never did have that kind of community. I hadn't ever really cruised gay bars, not engaged the abundant social media, hook-up sites. I'd gone to gay pride events sometimes. That was about the extent of it outside of voting correctly and donating money. I'd always met my partners (not that there have been many) in the course of my career, at a party, mostly just unplanned. But young gay men are connected in a myriad of ways these days, and I realized I needed to find someone to help me navigate if I were to see a pathway to Thomas's life. Former life. I had hoped Justin would be helpful, but he was still MIA. Jen had said she'd heard rumors that he was in Italy with some rich new boyfriend. I'd hoped that was the case. He'd given us a scare. Maybe Jen would have some other ideas.

She was not at the desk this morning. Adam? Adrien?—Damn it. What was his name?—was there along with another student assistant. "Good morning. I'm sorry, but I've forgotten your name..."

"That's okay. It's Will."

Will? What the hell? "Morning, Will. Do you know when Jen will be in?"

"She had an appointment today. She'll probably be in later, but I don't know when." He turned to the other assistant, who shrugged. Helpful.

"Tell her I'm looking for her if you see her, would you?"

"Sure." He went back to his phone, thumbing through pictures.

That gave me an idea. I found a relatively well-lit spot in the adjunct's shared office and laid the picture out on a desk. I took a few pictures of it with my cell phone, trying to get the focus as best as I could. I would send it to Jen, so she could ask around too. I pulled up her contact number and texted her a note with the picture. I put the picture in my desk drawer and headed off to class. When class was almost done, I felt my phone vibrate in my pocket. I waited until the students had all filed out, toting their mess of drawings and pads and toolboxes of drawing media. The text was from Jen: *Cool. I'll be a gumshoe.*

Where did she get this stuff?

I grabbed a takeout sandwich from the cafeteria. I thought I'd eat at my desk, catch up on phone calls and paperwork. I hadn't heard from Jake last night, but I figured he was probably hungover from Saturday night. I considered giving him a call, but I hesitated. He seemed to have taken on the role of first contact. Or was that a role I assigned him, my passivity playing a part. I punched his contact number. It rang until it went to voice mail. "Hey. Just me checking in. Call when you can."

After my last class, I headed home. The clouds had cleared, so it was colder, making the walk home a little slower. I hung my coat on the hook, and headed for the kitchen, kicking my shoes off at the bottom of the stairs and padding around in my socks. Clio rubbing in and around my ankle made walking precarious, so I snatched her up and walked her to her dishes. After dumping the disgusting mush they call cat food in her bowl and dropping her in front of it, I poured my two fingers of Lagavulin and sprawled out on the sofa for some bad TV watching. I got hungry around eight and threw a simple salad together. By ten, there was still no call from Jake. I did all the positive self-talk possible, without making myself nauseous, but could not deny the twinge of apprehension in my gut. I took myself to bed with a book and fell asleep with the light on.

And so the week passed. No hits from Jen on the picture. But she gave me a long explanation about the popular dating sites gay men used and how they worked; swipe right...swipe left...mind-boggling. No call from Jake. I'd left him another message on Wednesday, adding that I was a little worried. But nothing. As the days passed, my mood dimmed. I tried to think that even if nothing came of Jake and me, he'd brought me something: a confidence I didn't have before, maybe. So, determined to pass my days in something less than immobility, I joined the Y. I shopped online for a pair of trunks that were longish, slim, and a sedate navy. I had them shipped overnight, and by Friday, I was headed for the pool.

I used to swim a lot, before. I was a good swimmer, strong stroke, proper breathing. I was almost excited to get back to it. I lowered myself into the pool; it was virtually empty at midmorning. An elderly woman was in the next lane doing slow, steady laps. I'd stretched a little but warmed up by doing two laps of a slow breaststroke. Then I set into a crawl for laps. I kept a steady rhythm by choosing a song to sing to myself that matched the stroke speed I wanted to maintain. I chose "You Do Something to Me" and thought of Jake.

Chapter Fifteen

I didn't hear from Jake until Wednesday of the following week when I found him waiting for me on my front steps as I walked home from school. By then, of course, I knew. His expression confirmed it. "Jake." I stopped in front of him. God, I was sorry to lose him. But I was not going to make him feel bad. I was going to handle this disappointment with dignity; then I'd get drunk and break things. "Come in."

He followed me up the stairs and into the entryway, waiting as I turned on some lamps. He came in and stood awkwardly.

"Sit down," I said, a little impatient, just wanting to get it over with. I sat, and he followed. I on the sofa, he on the chair across. Deja vu. I waited.

"Sorry I didn't call, Ian. I wasn't sure what to say, and things were...changing. I didn't know where anything was gonna end up. I still don't." He stopped and shook his head. "That didn't make sense."

Suddenly, I just didn't want to hear any more. I didn't give a fuck what had happened. I didn't feel used or abused. I just felt exhausted. Jake didn't owe me anything. I didn't believe he was anything but sincere in his— what?—affection toward me. So, explanations, excuses, reasons, justifications just didn't matter to me. Before he could start again, I said, "Jake. You don't owe me anything. We had no understanding. If you have to go, go. It's okay."

"We always deserve explanations, don't we?" he asked, confused at my abruptness.

"Do we? I don't think so. I think they're for whoever is making them, not for others, not really," I said, a hint of resignation peeking through. "I mean, the bottom line is that you and I go forward, or we do not." I shrugged.

"Well, that's the thing. I'm kind of at a difficult point here in my life right now where I don't know which way to move. But I guess it would be that easy for you this time, go, don't go. There is no Arty for you now. Was it easy then?"

That brought me up. What was that supposed to mean? Was he still angry over what had happened? It seemed as though he'd gotten over it. 'There is no Arty...' Oh! Oh...

"There *is* someone waiting for you." Oh, hell.

"There wasn't when I told you that. He's not really waiting for me. Well, not in that way. Look, Ian, he and I were together for a long time before you and I reconnected. We'd broken it off six months or so before I saw you. We've been talking a little, and he came over that day you came by. I wasn't ready, wasn't sure I wanted to try with him again. He backed off for a while, but I saw him again the night I called you from the bar." He stopped abruptly and shoved the heels of his hands in his eyes and rubbed. "I'm feeling fucking stuck," he choked out. He looked up suddenly and said, "I didn't sleep with him, Ian. I haven't been seeing him. I just don't know what I want. I just think it's best, for me, anyway—" On that he chuckled a little. "—if I don't see anyone until I've figured it out. I'm not asking either of you to wait around. I take my chances that way, I know. But I don't think I can go forward, until this...these...until I'm less...confused."

He was done, I guessed. He was sitting forward on the chair, looking remorseful, pained. Inexplicably I got mad, ergo, sarcastic. "What an enviable conundrum to have two men who want you."

Jake looked at me evenly and said, "You must know what it feels like. You were in this position once. You tell me. Is it enviable?"

Fuck. I *was* in that position once. And I took the path of least resistance. I wondered what would have happened if I had stepped back and taken some time to think about what I'd really wanted; what would have been best for me. If I'd have known then what I knew now, I'd have picked Jake. Back then, when Arty became more present, I didn't think about my feelings. I didn't think about Jake's either. I didn't even consider that I had a choice. It was all about Arty. But I didn't say any of this to Jake. What I said was, "You're right. I was in your position. And I handled it badly. Chose badly."

"No, that's not what I'm trying to say. Not at all. Ian, I'm asking for a little time. I'm hoping you'll give it to me. I don't know where I'll end up. Maybe alone, but I just need a little time."

I nodded. It sounded so easy. A little time. But, even though I'd give him all the time in the world, if it wasn't me he chose, I'd likely slide back to where I was two, three months ago. I didn't say that either. "I can wait, Jake, for a little while" is what I said instead.

He nodded and said, "Thanks." Then he stood abruptly and headed out the door. He'd never taken his jacket off. I watched him walk down the street, his head bent, hands shoved into the pockets of his black leather bomber jacket, until he reached his Jeep. I closed the door, scratched at my knuckles, and thought about the best way to escape the pain.

*

I thought I was keeping it together reasonably well. I wasn't overdrinking. I was trying to stay busy, kept swimming, painted furiously. Both Jen and I had asked around about the mystery person. No one knew him. But we'd only asked around the campus. Providence was a big city. The photo had looked like a good lead on Thomas's life, or a piece of it, but I didn't know how to pursue it. I even considered hiring a private detective. I didn't think they would be under the same constrictions as the police, or Jake, anyway. After all, I would be a paying customer.

I was explaining my thought process to Fredrick one evening over dinner at his place when he asked if the guy looked like a student. I guessed he was. I'd assumed he was. Then he'd asked if I'd checked around other college campuses or any of the gay bars, maybe the bathhouses. I had to ask myself if I was that serious about it. It sounded kind of daunting. But, despite what Jake had said, it did feel as though the investigation was waning. I especially didn't want it to fade with me. I knew bathhouses were out. No way was I walking, naked, around a bunch of aroused men, asking them if they knew this guy. That'd get me nowhere but kicked out. But I could ask around at the bars. Fredrick asked me to text him the picture so that he could ask around too.

Fredrick helped me compile a list. I knew a few gay bars, but he knew them all, plus all the clubs. Fredrick offered to go with me, but I thought I might have more success alone. I also decided to do only three a night, starting with the farthest away and ending closer to home in case I ended up drunk. A distinct possibility these days. I was irrationally excited about this endeavor. I'd been feeling desolate, empty of desire to do anything but sleep. Or drink. Rita had been up a few times, not monitoring me, but cheerleading, or so she made it seem. Reminding me of my "inner strength" in taking a chance with Jake, regardless of the outcome. All very social work-y. I appreciated her efforts but preferred to just sit and watch movies with her. Her presence was filling and calming.

I chose a Friday night to start my venture. Dressed in jeans and a black long-sleeved T-shirt, I headed out around ten. Most of the bars are in the Down City and jewelry district. I began at Trinity Brewhouse. This was the one bar I was familiar with. Fredrick and I came here often. I sat at the bar and ordered a stout. Trinity is a little sedate for students, but I viewed it as a warmup, and a beer under the proverbial belt wouldn't hurt. The bartender was familiar, so I didn't feel funny asking him if he'd seen the young man. I used the picture on the phone. The original was better, but that seemed a little too much like *Law and Order*. As I expected, the barman didn't know him. I sat there and thought about whether I should start asking patrons. That seemed intrusive, but what did I care, really? I asked the bartender who the regulars were. He eyed me suspiciously but pointed out a few. I approached each of them and got the same 'What are you, a cop?' every time. I honestly, but briefly, filled them in on the story. None of them knew who the boy was. I asked if they knew Thomas. Got only *nos*. I finished my beer and headed to the next venue.

The night was warm for early March. The day had been sunny, around 50 degrees, and with the clouds moving in, some of the warmth was retained. I left my overcoat behind in the car for the next two bars. They were getting more and more crowded. It was clear that I should have started later in the evening. Repeating the same scenario, I had no luck at the next two places, and by then I was feeling irritated with loud music, unpleasantly tipsy, and hot. I went home. I decided that I would try one more time tomorrow night (or really, now, tonight) and then give up on this track.

I was saved by a text from Jen late Saturday morning.

HEY! Justin finally called me FROM ITALY. Asshole. Just wanted you to know.

Selfishly, I texted back.

Can you send picture of guy? See if he knows him? Did he know about Thomas?

Jen: *I told him about T. Was shocked. Asked if it was a customer. :-(I'll send photo in a text. Will let you know asap.*

Meanwhile, I headed upstairs to gesso a new canvas, while I called my favorite model, Damon, to see if he wanted to come tonight to sit. He said he could. I was standing in front of the unnatural white of the fresh gesso when my phone vibrated.

Jen: *He says he thinks this kid works at the Coffee Exchange.*

I shook my head at the improbability of the connection, but I was not about to discount it.

I was already dressed, so I just slipped into loafers and headed out. The Coffee Exchange is on Wickenden St. at the bottom of Benefit. I drove, though, not wanting to have to walk back up the hill to my house. I tried to temper my hope. Even if I found him, he may not be willing to talk. And what would I do with whatever it was he'd share with me? I didn't even know how meaningful it would be to know more. I just thought someone should.

Their parking lot was packed, so I knew it was going to be busy. The Coffee Exchange is a favorite in Providence, proven by the long line. It's in a charming little Empire-style house converted into a coffee shop, with local pastries and not nearly enough tables. As I walked in, I checked out the service people but didn't see anyone that could have been him. I got in line anyway, thinking I'd ask the barista when I ordered something. The line seemed to take forever to shrink, so by the time I got to the front, I'd decided I really did want a pastry with my coffee. I chose two pecan biscotti. While they were putting it together, I pulled out my phone and scrolled to the picture. When she brought my order I showed it to her, and she said immediately, "Hey, that's Stas. Nice picture."

I blinked at her and managed, "Is he around?"

"Sure. I think he's on break. Probably smoking around back."

I shoved the biscotti into my coat pocket, grabbed my coffee, and headed around to the back of the building. The young man was standing around the corner from a side rear door, smoking and talking on his cell phone. He was speaking a foreign language that sounded Slavic: Russian or Czech. He seemed annoyed and began just repeating "Katya! Katya!" Katya was not listening apparently. Wait. Katya? I stood back around the corner and waited until he'd finished. I walked toward him smiling.

"Katya, huh? Girlfriend troubles?" I tried to sound teasing, just an older guy teasing a kid.

He chuckled a little and said in a thick accent, "No, sister troubles." Huh.

"Ah. Listen, Stas, is it? I was a friend of Thomas Wilson's. I think you might have known him."

Stas looked startled and looked over my shoulder as if he expected others. "You are not with police are you?"

Now I was the one who looked startled. "No. I—look, my name is Ian Start. Like I said, I was a friend of his. I inherited his artwork, and there were a bunch of pictures of you. I just wanted to find someone who knew him. Someone who would maybe talk to me about him." I was sure I sounded completely insane.

He looked less startled, but wary, and a little sad, I thought. "You say you were a friend, but you want me to tell you about him," he said more as a challenge than a question, disconcerting that he hit on the source of my feelings of guilt.

"I was one of his art teachers." Oh, that would explain it. "I cared about him. It didn't seem to me that he had a lot of other people who did. I was hoping there were."

Stas looked at me for a long moment. He had blue-gray eyes, a steady, sure gaze, which suddenly welled, and as he flicked his cigarette butt into the back lot, I watched as the stub landed with a spray of tiny sparks. He said shortly, "There was," and then he pushed the back door open and disappeared. The butt lay there smoldering, and I contemplated stomping it out and picking up the filter. There were a million of its kin in the lot. I walked away letting it fester and pollute.

Well? What the hell did I expect? I expected to sit and reminisce about a dead young man with someone who didn't even know me. Sometimes I wonder what planet I am from. *Give it up, Start. Sometimes we don't get what we're looking for. Suck it up, and get on with your so-called life.* I went home.

Damon came around eight, and I set up lights, moved a chair over, and grabbed some props for him to use as I tested out different poses. Day, as we call him, was a regular model at RISD, and I use him often when I do figurative work. He is a dancer with the State Ballet of Rhode Island, but the troupe is only semiprofessional, which means he scrambles for money by waiting tables at the posher restaurants and modeling for artists. He has great stamina and can hold poses for an unnaturally long time. Starting with some gesture drawings to warm up, he struck a pose that I eventually came back to. He was walking away from me and stopped with head down and to the side, hands on his hips. It reminded me of the half glance back Jake had given me as he walked away. When Day struck that pose, I remembered Jake hesitating for just a second as he walked toward his car, and it seemed for a heartbeat, that he would turn back. But now I realized it was that pause of regret that we have when we know we've hurt somebody. That moment where we almost turn back and say "never mind" just to avoid causing someone pain. And when we do turn back, the end is only delayed. I thought then that although I'd wait, I would never see Jake again.

That's the painting I wanted: the brink of loss.

I spent a good deal of my time over the next week at my canvas, music on loud to try to fill the void. I felt as though there were pieces of puzzles floating around, waiting to be put in place, but were there many puzzles, or were the pieces all to one? Two, maybe three. My life was the more ambiguous puzzle. I'd lived to the near side of thirty with the feeling that I could accomplish whatever I chose. When that feeling blew up with the injury and Arty's betrayal, because that's how I'd come to see it, I'd felt utterly adrift. I didn't like that my art often came from so far within that I was unconscious of it. It scared me. The nudes were more conscious, enjoyable. I loved them. I pushed boundaries, edges. But the more abstracted ones, the dogs—those were the ones I lost myself in. And I missed writing terribly, more loss. The recent interlude with Jake felt like it was a push along a healthier track, but did I want a healthier track to be based on a relationship with another? If there weren't external impetuses to regain missing parts of my "self" or my art, where or what were the internal impulses? Was the absence of answers the same as the lack of puzzle pieces? Can one buy puzzle pieces?

My mind wandered to what I'd found out about Thomas's friend, Stas. When I'd overheard him on the phone behind the coffee shop, he'd been talking to a Katya. What were the chances this was Pearson's Katya? It's not that I don't believe in coincidences—of course, there are—it's a big disordered world. But it didn't feel coincidental. I tried to sort it out by what I knew: Katya is sleeping with Pearson, she, maybe, has a brother, Stas. Stas knew Thomas at least somewhat intimately. Okay. So what? I started again. Pearson had something with Thomas, Pearson was rich. No, not rich, rich wife on whom he may be dependent for an artistic livelihood. He was weird about the portfolio. If his wife found out he might be really screwed. I, again, entertained the idea that he feared being blackmailed. If it did happen, would it point to Thomas? That didn't feel right. And that's where I got stuck.

I was discussing it all with Rita one Sunday morning. Bouncing ideas back and forth. "So, Pearson might have a reasonable fear of being blackmailed, but has he been? How can we know?" she asked.

"I wonder if the police know." I considered calling Jake to just ask, but I didn't want him to think I had ulterior motives for calling. I wondered if Ransom would tell me. I doubted it. Would Pearson tell me? He might. But asking might push him past his self-control, considering how he came at me a few weeks ago. If he were being blackmailed, he'd probably lie to me anyway. Would he not lie to someone else? Who? Katya? I ran all of this by Rita.

"I don't know. Maybe Katya. But I don't see how you could ask her. Anyway, the fact that Katya may have a brother who knew Thomas seems so...out there. Why do you want to know if he's being blackmailed again?" She shook her head like she was trying to clear it.

"I want to know it wasn't Thomas." I sighed. Rita sighed. We sipped our coffee. Thought.

"Do you think this Stas could be involved? Maybe he knew about the portfolio and the affair. Maybe he had something to do with it. Maybe Thomas didn't even know he did," she offered.

I looked at Rita. "What if I just asked him straight out? If he lies, which I assume he will if he's guilty, what would I look for?"

Rita guffawed. "Like, is there a pamphlet on telling whether people lie or not? You can't tell for sure. If he's good at it, you won't know; if he's not, you will. Does that help?"

"Absolutely," I joked back.

"Seriously, Ian. I don't think a blackmailer will take kindly to being asked about it. It could make him or her a little testy."

"Her," I stated. My thoughts went to Katya, but that made no sense either.

"And why are you pursuing this again?" Rita put her jaw in her hand, elbow on the table, eyebrow raised.

"Not." I shrugged. "Just conjecture. Bored." Why was I? Puzzle pieces. I wanted to know what happened. No. I was pursuing this. I wanted to know who killed him. There. I admitted it to myself. Did I really think I'd solve it over the police? I didn't. But I thought maybe standing in a different spot and therefore getting a different view might make a difference. "You know what I'll do? I'll ask Katya if she has any family here in the U.S. That might lead to something. It's just an innocent question, right?" Rita shrugged me a worried look.

Chapter Sixteen

The next day I hung around the office to see if Katya came by. I'd told Jen earlier that I'd talked to the mystery boy. I'd also asked her if she'd ever heard Katya talk about or to anyone named Stas. She laughed and said that Katya spoke Russian on her phone a lot to someone, that all words sounded like "Stas" in that language, but she'd try to keep an ear open.

I sat in my office feeling antsy, tapping a pen, trying not to scratch at my finger joints, unable to concentrate on administrative paperwork. Jen finally yelled "Stop it" to me. I got up and told her I was going for a walk, would she please text me if Katya showed up.

I headed down Benefit St. walking and thinking. The weather was sunny and fortyish, so I walked with my overcoat open. I peered at the stately homes along the street, some converted to lawyer's offices, realtors. I was longing for spring, warm and green, the smell of the ocean rife and beckoning. I found that I'd strolled down to Wickenden. I turned left and headed for the Coffee Exchange. If Stas was there, maybe I'd try to talk to him again.

He wasn't at the counter when I got my tea. I didn't ask for him. I sat reading a paper or looking at the words as my thoughts ran unchecked. It occurred to me that if Katya was blackmailing Pearson, did she kill Thomas? Did she have a motive? Someone knew about the portfolio besides Pearson and me and Thomas, of course. That person hit me over the head hard enough to do damage and stole it. Stas could know about it. As if my thoughts conjured him, Stas sat down across from me.

"What are you doing here?" It was an accusation made a little sinister by his heavy Slavic accent. I wondered if Russians always assumed the worst in any situation. "What do you want?"

"I came for a tea. What I want is to talk about Thomas a little." I sighed. "He took some really nice photos of you. You two were close, I think." I didn't ask, didn't want to give him room to squirm out of it.

Stas looked at me for a moment, assessing. "I'm gay. You have a problem with gays?"

I laughed. "Not hardly."

He nodded. "I met him at a bar. We liked each other. He was a nice guy. In Russia, it is hard to be with men. We get beat up a lot." He smiled crookedly. "He was my first American friend. He was a good friend." He looked down at the table, but I could see through his dark lashes the tears caught there.

"Stas, do you have any idea why someone would kill him?" I asked quietly.

His head shot up like I'd accused him. "Is that why you're here? I thought you were not with police."

"No. I'm not with the police. I was just a teacher of his. The police talked to you though."

"They say they are talking to everyone who knows Thomas. Asked where I was. About me coming from Russia, me being gay, having a relationship with Thomas. Other stuff I don't think has anything to do with Thomas." His tone was hostile. I could hear the distrust of police, authority, answering questions. I'm a little worldly. I knew that living in Russia was a nightmare for most people, more for homosexuals, I imagined. Being truthful and forthcoming with police probably didn't work out for the populous very often.

I leaned in a little conspiratorially, smiled knowingly, and said, "Did you tell them everything?"

He looked at me like I was an idiot. "Mostly, yes. But I say I don't have family here. I don't want police to talk to them."

"Your sister." He looked at me, confused. "'Sister trouble' remember?"

"Oh, yeah." Stas squirmed in his hard chair a little.

"They probably know about her. Last name and all. She goes to RISD right?" I took a chance with this question.

"She has different last name." Okay. He didn't deny the RISD connection. There is a connection here. I could feel it. Taste it. My heart started to beat faster, and I wondered if I was going to have a panic attack, but I wasn't done.

"Stas, I'm glad Thomas had someone who cared about him, really. But I think it might be that he got into some trouble concerning a teacher at school. I think they were close, then something happened. There were some drawings. Did he say anything about it to you?"

Stas hesitated and said cautiously, "I saw drawings. He told me a little. Nothing bad. But I don't tell police about it. That is private for Thomas."

"Stas, the police think he was a prostitute. That's how he paid for his apartment, his art supplies, food. Did you know this?"

Stas looked pained as he shook his head. "I did not like that he did that. He said he did it back home after his aunt died. He lived on the streets, tricked, and finished high school. No one knew he was not at home. He was all alone. There he says he had to; here he says he chooses to. To me, no choice; had to. He had no money. No family. Both places." He wiped his eyes quickly and looked up, meeting my eyes as if looking for a final judgment. He didn't find it.

I just nodded and asked, "Look, do you want some of his artwork? The photographs?"

He looked at me, his eyes bright. "Yes. Thank you. Yes."

"Good. Give me your number. I'll give you mine. We can get together one day, and you can go through all of it, decide what you want." He nodded and gave me his number. So he'd have mine, I texted him: *It was nice to meet you.*

On impulse, I asked, "Stas, were you around when he got beat up last year?"

Stas nodded and said, "He wouldn't tell me who did it. Wouldn't go to doctor. Just said he was okay, to forget about it." He shrugged in futility.

We agreed to talk sometime the following week and said goodbye. I headed back up the hill for my afternoon class.

*

That evening, reclining on my sofa, cat on my lap, and scotch at hand, Jake's admonishments about not poking around haunted me. I considered whether Stas was involved in any of this outside of his relationship with Thomas. And while I, as I said, allow for coincidences, I did not think the relationship string between Stas, Katya, and Andrew Pearson was one. The idea that Katya was blackmailing Pearson didn't stall based on her personality, as it did with Stas. But would a blackmailer have a continued affair with her victim? For how long? Logistically, it could be done if the victim didn't know who the blackmailer was, I supposed. The blackmailer would have to have some tangible proof of the indiscretion. I would have thought it was the portfolio, only that would lead back to Thomas. Katya didn't have it. Not then anyway. Does she have it now? Did she hit me over the head? Did she have the strength to hit me hard enough to knock me out? The height? Stas certainly did. Maybe he was just a terrific actor. As for Thomas, he hung around the office regularly and did not seem noticeably uncomfortable around Pearson. Would a blackmailer do that? I tried to remember any interchanges between the two and could not. I couldn't remember Pearson and Thomas in the same place at all, as a matter of fact. Clearly, Thomas hadn't been living rich anyway. And if he had been successfully blackmailing Pearson, he wouldn't have been tricking.

I continued to mull over the possibility that Stas was involved, but he never balked about talking to me about the drawings or that Thomas had been involved with a teacher. He didn't tell the police what he knew, but there was a strong possibility that it was due to some cultural paranoia. Rita and I had once had a discussion about that concept. She described it as an "often life-saving, all-encompassing distrust of the authority that systematically represses a race or class." I could see that in Stas's case. It also occurred to me that these two individuals probably had no interest in returning to Russia. I wondered what their immigration status was. Katya was most likely on a student visa. I didn't know if Stas was a student. He was working in a coffee shop, so he wasn't here because he had a sought-after skill set.

"Be careful," Jake had said. I probably hadn't been. It was exciting trying to fit pieces into the puzzle. I could see why he loved his job. My mood suddenly dropped. Sometimes the thought of him could suck me down a whirlpool. I missed him. I missed the thrill of the start of a new relationship with him. It had felt so right. I thought he'd felt it, too, but I guessed that it was naive to think that every partnering is equal in the depth of emotion. I knew that I'd fallen fast. Too fast. I'd smothered him.

I fell asleep on the sofa at the end of Maria Callas singing, "Ah, Fors'e Lui Che L'anima." I didn't dream of dogs. I dreamt of soft full lips, warming caresses, tender whispers.

Chapter Seventeen

"I'm not going back to Russia because of one disgusting little faggot! My life is shit there. I'd have to marry some fat alcoholic asshole to survive there," Katya hissed, spittle hitting my coat.

How the hell did it get to this? I'd gone to teach classes on Wednesday as usual. I'd made another vow to stay out of the whole debacle. I needed to focus on keeping my own life together and the distraction of Thomas, Stas, Pearson, and Katya was just that—a distraction. And dangerous things were going on, not the least of which was a murder. I was on my way out of my office; it was late, and no one else was there. I had my coat on when Katya charged in. She pushed me back into my office and shut the door. She pulled a gun out of a canvas tote and told me to sit down with my hands where she could see them. I complied; it seemed prudent.

"You talked to my brother. Why?" Anger was turning her fair skin plum.

"Jesus, Katya. What the hell are you doing? Put that away. I talked to your brother. I didn't know he was your brother until this week. What's the problem?" I had a hunch I knew what the problem was—Stas must have told her about meeting me. He also must know a little more than what he told me. Or Katya knew precisely what was going on, and Stas had shared with me more than what Katya was comfortable with.

"What do police know? And don't say you don't know. I see you kiss that cop." What the fuck? Was she spying on me? Where would she have seen...oh, right. At Harry's, when Jake kissed me.

I was about to explain that I wasn't seeing Jake anymore, and he had never discussed Thomas's murder with me. But what came out of my mouth was "Did you kill Thomas?"

"Is this what police think?" Absurdly, given the state of my terror, I wanted to tell her she was getting clumsy with her articles, but I reconsidered the wisdom of it. "You tell police I kill Thomas? Asshole! You ruin everything! I get money to bring my brother here, but you people make him into a queer. He was fine in Russia—he liked girls— he comes here, meets that little fag, and he ruins him. Disgusting. You should have minded your own business." I couldn't pull my stare away from her eyes. They were insane-looking, open wide, whites showing all the way around. Her face was contorted in rage, spit gathered in the corner of her mouth, making webs when she spoke.

"*You're* blackmailing Pearson. You knew about the drawings. That they had a relationship." I instantly regretted opening my mouth.

"Andrew is an idiot. I get money from him. He is very rich and doesn't want his wife to know he is perverted. He thinks that boy was blackmailing him. Stupid, but very handy, that boy. You figure this all out by yourself, or do police know?"

"Then *you* killed Thomas."

"No! No reason to. He was more use to me alive. Is this what you tell police?" She was getting shrill. I hoped there was someone out there hearing this.

"I don't know what the police know." Was this the right answer? Or would it get me killed?

"Ah, good. This is good, Ian." I didn't like her tone, as though we were good friends. "I have to make sure you don't tell them about Stas, okay? Now he knows too much." She sounded almost sad as she raised the pistol. "And he is so weak."

"You're going to shoot me right here?" My heart was racing, and I insanely imagined having a panic attack, falling to the floor, gasping, sweating, shaking in front of a crazy, armed woman. Maybe I should do just that. But then, maybe she would just shoot me right here like an injured horse.

"Fuck no. You're coming with me. I'll kill you somewhere else." *Oh. Good. Much better.* She signaled for me to walk ahead of her. We reached an outer door at the end of the hall. It was one we could exit from but was locked to the outside. Nearing dark, the sky was a deep violet—the time of evening where all light seems to be sucked into a void. The street was lit up but unusually empty and quiet. *She could kill me right here and now and walk away unseen, then step back into the building unobserved.* But she stepped out behind me and indicated that I should head straight into the street. I saw the gun was raised but held close to her body, partially hidden in the folds of her unbuttoned wool coat. I stepped off the curb into the street.

From behind a car, across the street and to my right, I heard Ransom's voice: "Katya Veselovsky. Police. Hands up, and get on the ground." I looked around just as Katya aimed the gun away from me toward the voice and shot twice, the blast so near my ears that I was instantly deafened. Before I could dive behind a car on my side of the street, away from Katya, I saw Jake fly back from behind the hood of a car across the street, in a spray of blood. And then I didn't care what happened. I heard a muffled *pop-pop-pop* of gunshot through my ringing ears as I was running as best I could toward Jake. Ransom was crouched behind the car beside him, looking over toward where Katya had been standing, his gun still up and pointing. I didn't see where she was. I was looking at Jake.

Christ! He'd been shot in the side of his neck. Blood was pouring out of the back making a puddle beneath him. His eyes were open, not focusing but moving. He wasn't dead. "Jake, Jake, Jake." I was muttering over and over. I couldn't hear myself. I didn't know what to do. Pressure. Pressure on a wound. I reached behind him and tried to feel for an exit wound. Blood poured over my hand, warm, thick. The coppery smell of blood and the acrid odor of gunfire wafted for a moment but was blown away by a breeze. "How do I stop the bleeding? Ransom! How do I stop this?" Ransom had run over to where Katya was lying, flailing around, cursing. He was handcuffing her and talking on his cell phone at the same time.

Desperate, I kept searching until I found the exit wound. I ripped my scarf off and pressed against the gaping wound as best I could. The front started to ooze, and with a bare hand I bore down on that too. He was still breathing. "It's okay, Jake. Help's coming; help's coming, love." His eyes fluttered. Shut. But he was still breathing, looking an unholy shade of ivory, and he was starting to shake. *Please, please, please, please* was my mantra. And the blood continued to ooze through the scarf, between my fingers, around my hands. Ransom was there now, and other police officers were showing up. Someone wanted to take my place, but I wouldn't let go; he couldn't spare the blood. Then someone shoved clean towels at me, and I pressed them against the flow.

Ransom said something I couldn't hear. I shook my head. He shouted, "It's not spurting, I think that's good." I shook my head again. *There is nothing "good" about this.*

After a frigging week, the ambulance showed up. The paramedics had to pry my hands away; it was as though they were frozen to Jake, glued, and I couldn't have let him go on my own. I stood and watched, not registering what I was doing, just watching his face, noting every sign of life. It was then I started bargaining with a God I didn't believe in. *Tell me what you want, and I'll do it. I'll let him go, never see him again if you let him live. I'll do it. Is that what you want?*

They spent a long time working on him, packing his neck, hooking up an IV, a defibrillator, talking to the hospital, reporting his vitals, a long conversation about not intubating because of the neck wound. They were wasting time! I wanted him in a hospital, now. Ransom seemed okay with it though. He asked a question now and then and waited patiently. One of the uniforms came over to get a statement from me, but Ransom told him it could wait for a bit.

Finally, after an hour, though in all actuality it was probably only minutes since they arrived, they slid a board under him, then lifted that onto a wheeled cot. I watched as Ransom got in with them, and they drove off. Before he left, he'd told me he'd keep me posted. I stood in the middle of the street, numb. I started to shiver. I felt nauseous, dizzy. I headed back to the curb and sat down hard, putting my head between my legs. One of the cops came over and asked if I wanted one of the EMTs from the second ambulance to check me out, his voice coming from miles off. I shook my head. I had an urge to put the heels of my hands in my eyes, but my palms were covered in blood. It was everywhere: soaked up my cuff, over the front of my overcoat, the puddle where his head had lain. The tears came, unstoppable.

The cop sat next to me. "Let's do a brief statement; then you can come in tomorrow, and we'll do a formal statement, okay?" I nodded.

"What happened here?" I asked as I swept my arm across the chaotic panorama that still remained. I felt disconnected, as though I were in a movie scene. It was almost hyperreal. My mind jumped to photorealism and hyperrealism. Which was this? It wasn't mundane: no gas station, blue-plate-special cafe, muscle cars, or vanitas. But it was beyond even hyperrealism. And it occurred to me how constructed art is, only stabbing at what we feel and what we fear. Christ. I think this shit now?

"I guess her brother called Ransom and told him his sister had gone berserk after she found out he'd talked to you. She grabbed her gun and told the kid she was going to kill you. He believed her. They, Ransom and Quinn, were first on scene. They called it in, but when they saw her come out with you, they had to act."

Jesus. This was my fault. I had to stick my nose in, poke and prod, exacerbate, irritate, and so I had to make this right. Somehow. I stood. "I'll come in tomorrow, okay? Who should I ask for?"

"I'll leave your name at the desk. They'll know who to call. You want a lift home?"

"No. I have to finish something up here first."

He looked at me, my bloodied hands, coat, and then shrugged and went back to the knot of cops on the other side of the street. I headed back past them to the main door on the square. There were two cops there keeping people from leaving and going in. The officer I'd just been talking to signaled to them to let me in. I stopped at the restroom to wash my hands, watching Jake's blood swirl uselessly down the drain. Back in the office, there was still no one at the desk, but Pearson's desk light was on. I went in and shut the door. He looked up and saw my stained coat. In the lamplight he probably couldn't tell it was blood. My coat sleeves covered my stained shirt cuffs.

"What's up with the cops out front? The whole place is locked down."

I stood over him, exhausted and angry, frankly wanting him to give me a reason to injure him. "Tell me what happened between you and Thomas. And so help me, if you don't tell me the truth, I will know it, and I will ruin you."

He met my eyes for a change. He put down his pen and turned his chair toward me. There was an uncomfortable pause during which I thought he was waiting for me to start the conversation. I did not. I stood there, silent. "I'm not gay," he finally offered, as if that would be enough. I shrugged. "Twice in my life, God put men in front of me that were beyond temptation." He sighed and rubbed his hands over his face as if to wipe away his sins, his reticence. "One who I taught myself to hate." He gave me a long look and started to say something, then seemed to change his mind. His gaze was weighty. With a growing feeling of despair, I knew, then, the reason he loathed me. He broke the stare. "The other was of such...beauty and perfection"—he frowned as if in pain—"I could only...have. Had to have. I took. It's a sickness, you know. I saw this...this...stunning boy, and I couldn't stop myself. I didn't want to stop myself. It was—is a disgusting affliction, a weakness, an obsession. I hated myself for it. Hate myself for it." I didn't think he was really conscious of who he was talking to in that moment. His eyes were focused on some distant point that did not exist. Not in the confines of the office.

"Jesus, Pearson. This is not an illness. We love who we love. Are attracted to who we are attracted to. Besides, he was just a boy. What happened?" My ears continued to ring loudly, and I was feeling unsteady, so I swiped the papers off his guest chair and sat.

Refocusing on me, he said, "It may please you to think that Thomas was an innocent young man, but I assure you, he wasn't." Pearson sat straighter in his seat as he said this, and he looked like a preacher: that sanctimony reserved for the self-righteous. "The little whore was blackmailing me, Start. He was threatening to tell my wife, the college. It would have ruined me. Ruined my family. And don't talk to me about homosexuality not being an illness. Only a sick person would do that. Fuck someone and then blackmail them. I see how he sucked me in... I beat him and he still denied it, still didn't stop." He was standing by now, spluttering in his outrage. He made me tired, tired of treading through this life with the fatuous, the psychopaths. It was too much. I stood.

"What is going on outside is that Katya was just arrested by the police. She was the one who was blackmailing you." I didn't want to see his face. But I looked him in the eye and said: "She admitted it to me. I just spent the last hour dealing with the consequences. The police know."

Pearson sat down hard in his chair, the force carrying it back on its wheels. "That's bullshit." He stared at me belligerently, as though I should back down or change my story. "No. That can't be right. She wouldn't do that. It was Thomas. Even Katya knew it was him."

"She did it. She found out about the portfolio from her brother, who knew Thomas. She knew you, how you sleep with your students. Tell me, did she seduce you, or did you seduce her?" I didn't wait for an answer. I saw it in his expression, something less self-assured. "She realized that you'd do anything to protect your place in your wife's financial pocket. She did it, Pearson, not Thomas. She just led you to believe it was him. She told me, Andrew, just now."

His face slowly imploded into a grisly contortion, horror in his eyes. "Oh, Jesus, oh God, no. No, no, no, no, no." Pearson keened into his hands, and suddenly I got it.

"Oh fuck, Andrew. What have you done?"

He didn't move, save his head, which he rocked back and forth in his hands. He abruptly started to sob, great gasping and ugly noises escaped from between his palms. I waited for the words, but they didn't come.

"*You* did it, didn't you? You killed him." He finally looked up, tears and snot dripping an ugly testimony.

"Get out, Start. Get out." His tone was weary, defeated.

"I'm going to go get a cop. Do. Not. Leave." As if I had some control over this world. I left and headed down the hall to the door where I'd seen the two officers stationed. Just as I reached for the handle, I heard *BLAM* from down the hall. The two officers looked at each other, startled, and then at me. They opened the door and headed the way I was pointing, down the same hall I'd just come from. I followed reluctantly.

He'd not closed the door. The cops were standing at the threshold, one of them talking into his radio. I could only see Andrew's left arm and an awkwardly crumpled leg on the dark gray carpeting, but the blood had splattered everywhere.

Chapter Eighteen

I walked home in a daze, but the cold air did me some good. As I walked along the water, I let the soft whoosh of the river along the concrete urge me along. I still felt detached from what had happened. After spending another two hours talking to the police, the only thing registering in a tangible way was the memory of Jake's body falling backward, and the warmth of his blood. The backs of my knees twinged at the thought.

Once home, I quickly showered, tucked my beloved, now bloodied, overcoat and the shirt in a trash bag, and put it in the bin outside. I threw on a clean sweater, got in my car, and headed to the hospital. I had not heard from Ransom.

In the emergency waiting area, I headed for the desk and told the woman I was there for Jake Quinn. She asked if I was family. I told her I was his cousin. She said there was a family member and a police detective in the family waiting room and showed me how to get there. Ransom was sitting with a good-looking young man, heads close together, talking. He saw me and shook his head slightly, so I stopped. At first, I thought he was trying to tell me Jake didn't make it, and my heart slammed in my chest. But after a second, I got it. This was Chris. Christian. Maybe my bargain had been fulfilled. I turned to go, but I couldn't make myself leave, not without knowing, so I sat in a chair on the other side of the room. I pulled my phone out conspicuously and waited.

Not long afterward, I saw Ransom tapping on his phone. I turned off my vibrate and sound and waited. It lit up.

He went in for evaluation, CT scans, etc. May go straight to surgery from there. Very Critical. Waiting for Dr.

Oh, thank God, still alive. I looked away, out the window, not seeing. I texted back.

Thanks. Will wait. Won't cause trouble.

He looked over, and I met his eyes. He looked sorry. He looked worried. We all looked worried. We all loved him.

Maybe fifteen minutes later, a doctor in scrubs came in, and Ransom and Chris stood up to talk to him. They listened, nodded, listened, nodded. Fuck. Me. The doctor left. They sat down. They talked. I could only hear a few quiet murmurs. Ransom glanced at me once. He then pulled his phone out. Chris asked him something, and Ransom answered. Ransom's fingers tap, tap, tapped.

He is in surgery. Still very critical. Much blood loss, which is the worst of it. Expected to survive surgery, not perfect odds for recovery. Hope for best. Go home.

I looked up and shook my head. I could not leave. How could I?

We sat like that for hours. One or the other would get up to relieve one's self, get coffee, pace. Otherwise, we all sat. There were others who came, stayed a long time, talked to doctors, left or were admitted to the hospital's depths. I don't know if Chris noticed that no one came to speak to me. I didn't care. After two more hours, four total, the same doctor came back in. Again, Chris and

Ransom stood. The same infuriating routine. Nod, listen... They sat. Ransom texted.

Muscle and tissue damage. Right interior jugular vein severed. Not anterior, which is good. Reparable. Still in surgery. Still critical. Maybe another hour.

I texted.

Okay. Thanks. Will wait...

It was another hour and a half before the routine repeated itself like a movie scene on a loop. This time Ransom gave a half smile. That was good, right? Ransom texted.

Out of surgery. Be in post-op for an hour at least, then to ICU. Will be kept heavily sedated for a while. Will be touch and go next few days. We are going home for a few hours. You do same. I will let you know if anything changes.

I nodded, watched them leave and continued to stare out the window into the black. I knew I didn't belong there. Chris was there for him now, the decision clearly made, but I couldn't leave. I'd gotten this man shot. My cavalier attitude throughout this whole ordeal came back in a wave of regret. From the moment Thomas was killed, there were incidents that should have scared me off: I was robbed, I got hit over the head, the portfolio was taken, Pearson threatened me. And I just kept trotting blindly, obliviously along. Then Jake had to save my life. And as a result, nearly was killed.

As the night turned to morning, according to the clock, not the sun, the area quieted. I was the only one in the waiting room. No one came to inform me of anything, and I began to get restless. I stepped into the hallway, thinking I would go home but was disoriented in which way the exit was. I looked left and saw a door with a sign that said ICU. I quietly cracked open the swinging door and saw a nursing station. No one was there. I went in and began the circuit of darkened rooms. They were arranged like rays around the nucleus of the nurses' arced counter, most doors standing open. Some were empty, but for those that were not, the patient's face was in the dark, impossible to make out features unless I went in. One room was lit, and I heard some rustling and soft voices. Nurses. I ducked back into the room I'd just come out of and waited. I told myself that the worst that could happen was they'd have me escorted out, but that didn't stop my heart rate from escalating. They finished and shut out the light, heading back to the nurses' station.

When their backs were turned, I slipped into the next room and found my way to the head of the bed. It was Jake. The clicks, the whirls, the soft beeps of the sustaining equipment were the only sounds. The rise and fall of his chest coincided with the tock and wheeze of a machine. Screens cast an unnatural green on the side I was on, so I moved to the other to stay in the dark. I stood back against the wall and watched him breathe. In. Out. In. Out. There was a short round stool on wheels to the side, which I eventually sat on and quietly wheeled to the edge of his bed. Taking his hand I whispered, "I'm sorry, love." I watched his chest rise and fall, hypnotic, reassuring.

Someone was tapping me on my back. I must have dozed, my arm had gone to sleep. I'd been using it to cushion my head from the bed rails. "What are you doing in here?" she whispered. "You shouldn't be in here. Who are you? A relative?" I shook my head and sat back on the stool.

"No. I'm a friend. Ian Start. I'll go." I stood, letting go of Jake's hand. I leaned over and kissed his head, brushed his wiry hair and whispered next to his ear, "Thank you, Jake" and left.

*

I was on a night's shore of black sand marred by rounded boulders of pitted lava rock that extended into the nearly black and viridian sea. Twenty feet out was a majestic throne-like chair sitting on the water's surface. I must get to the chair. The chair was for me, my due, my reward for something unknown, unexpressed, that felt ultimately undeserved. Reaching this cathedra felt imperative. I started stepping from boulder to black boulder, the rough rock abrading my bare feet. I had to reach down from time to time to catch my balance and the razor-like pits sliced at my hands. I finally reached the chair and sat, exhausted but relieved. Without warning, the chair began to sink. I felt betrayed. I'd made it to this lofty place, and now I would drown? Unable to leave the chair (Was I tied?), I took a breath just before the seat lowered into the salty gloom. I convinced myself this must be an educational ride. It was about the undersea world, and I should open my eyes, see the wonders, but I couldn't. I was blind and running out of air in a false realm...

I woke up gasping.

*

In the morning, I canceled classes for the rest of the week and lay in a little. I spent four hours at the police station, interviewed by three different cops, all in plain clothes;

none were Ransom. None were sharing information on Jake, or Katya, or Pearson, for that matter, although I was directed to tell them the details of the conversations I'd had with her and Pearson again and again. I signed a paper and was finally allowed to leave.

Over the next few weeks, I struggled to maintain a halfway normal life. I bugged Ransom for updates on Jake, and he always patiently obliged. Jake was making steady progress. After a few days under heavy sedation, they let him start coming around and were able to remove the breathing tube. Then there was a mild but persistent infection that was worrisome and so back on a breathing apparatus. It finally resolved, and eventually, they moved him to a regular hospital room. He was still weak, Ransom said, but stable.

I'd gone, then, one afternoon, to see him. I was given his room number and headed up in an elevator to his floor. His door was open, and I could hear a man talking, joking. I stopped a few feet outside the room. I could see that Jake was sitting somewhat upright, smiling, with Chris sitting on his bed. Jake caught my eye just as I was turning to leave. I had no time to read his expression. I vowed not to go back. Maybe I'd write him a letter.

So, my life reverted back in some semblance to pre-Jake. In some ways, I was less depressed. But I was sad. Rita and Fredrick were around more, and I appreciated that. I needed them, wanted them around more than before. Jake had opened the idea of possibilities for me, and I felt profound gratitude for that, and for these two friends who'd stood by me unfailingly through narcissistic tantrums, illness, depression, drunkenness. I often found myself portraying a more contented mien than I actually felt, but the alternative felt regressive. Fredrick made me go to a bar a couple of times and insisted that I practice flirting a little. I was awkward and ultimately hilarious. But I didn't want a hookup. I kept myself from wanting anything.

Ransom had let me know when Jake was discharged and then sort of signed off, as if saying his duty was done. One day, I checked my phone messages and found that Jake had called. His message said he wanted to talk to me when I had a free moment, but I opted to spare us both more pain and deleted it. There were times when I thought this disconnect was for the best anyway. Parts of me were still so unhealed, unhealthy. Parts of me were still missing. And now my night terrors were of blood loss and losing Jake to death.

Ransom had also updated me on the Katya debacle. He said there were indications that she'd blackmailed Russian men to get here, and she was wanted for questioning in the death of a man over there. Once here, it appeared as though she extorted a few other men. Katya used the money for school, to bring over some of her family, and to pay for bribes to get them out of that country. A local journalist wrote an article on her and her life as a deprived girl born in one of the most impoverished areas of Russia. He'd written that she was described by family members as a precocious and aggressive child. Defiant and always in trouble, she'd pushed the rigid boundaries in her home country blah, blah, blah. I couldn't muster sympathy in the face of the catastrophe she wrought. There was nothing on Pearson except an obit that cited a long battle with depression. Money spoke when one needed to hush, I supposed. There was no mention of Thomas Wilson. His murder was solved, I knew, but to the little world I occupied in

Providence, Rhode Island, his name only rested now with a few. His short life a blip in a bigger, meaner world than he had ever bargained for.

I'd kept in touch with Stas. He was cleared of any wrongdoing, and he'd found a pro bono lawyer to help him stay in the country. He'd come one afternoon to sort through Thomas's artwork. He took all of the photos of himself, and a few beautiful figurative paintings. We sat drinking tea for a while, and he talked about their relationship, about Thomas's life before Providence. Thomas had come so far on his own. He'd finished high school on his own, without a parent to wake him, make him brush his teeth, wear clean clothes. He managed to do this regardless of whether he was on the street or staying with a friend in order to keep out of the system. *How incredibly resourceful and strong! What a terrible loss.*

Spring was approaching, and I was sitting outside on a warmish afternoon, admiring the garden cleanup I'd started. Soggy leaves were raked into a pile and brown paper bags were filled with weeds and dead flower heads. The damp umber earth, musty and rich, hinted at a future, and I was feeling content in the moment as I let the sun warm my face and shine alizarin through closed eyes. I had been painting steadily recently, with less of a detached state, more intentionally. I'd made a contact in Boston a year or so ago, an owner of a gallery who'd expressed interest in my work. He'd called a few months ago to see if I had enough work for a decent show, and I said I thought I did. The nudes were finished—they'd show well—hopefully, sell. I held back the one I thought of as Jake. I could at least have that. The opening was set for the following month, which left only a few weeks for a few more to be dry enough to hang.

*

Openings are generally dreadful. They attract a lot of art students looking for free food and wine. I get it. Money's tight for many of them. We did the same as students. Boston is a town where there are a few more sophisticated or at least articulate art show goers than in Newport, and I have a small reputation up there. But there are always the artsy types who just want to be seen. They have no genuine interest in, or love of art. They take artists' statements seriously and then take exception to them, or they want to discuss philosophy or theory, or they ask if I can draw or paint realistically or why I don't title my paintings. Dressing in their most expensive casual wear to look like they could belong anywhere, *tres de rigueur*. They "go up my ass sideways" as they say around here. But if one shows, one has to suck it up and smile and try to answer civilly and hope it means a sale or two. And it's not all bad, sometimes friends and colleagues show up.

I was finishing up a conversation with a frail-looking, but intrusive, elderly man with a fake British accent who had been asking me why I didn't have an artist's statement. I was explaining to him that I thought the vast majority of artists' statements came after the creation of a work or a body of work and that the artist looked back to try to make sense of it. To me, that was personal. And I wanted viewers to have their own reasons for their response to my art. That was part of the beauty of art: the extraordinary variety of reactions. He was unsatisfied and was trying to explain to me that I needed a theory behind my creations, a place to come from, speak from. I was responding to that bullshit when I saw, in an adjoining section of the gallery, the back of a familiar tawny head. I excused myself and took a few steps toward him. I waited to see if he would be joined by anyone, but he moved from picture to picture alone, occasionally commenting to a stranger standing at the same painting. The din of the gallery chatter kept me from hearing anything. He lingered in front of the nudes. He talked to the gallery assistant as he looked at one of them. He spent longer looking at the dogs, his back to me, so I couldn't see his expression.

As he made the U-turn around the section, he spotted me watching him. He beamed his beautiful, vulnerable, open smile and headed over. I was smiling back.

"Ian," he said.

"Jake," said I.

Chapter Nineteen

It was a good show, busy enough, though I probably only sold a few paintings: the nudes. After all, those who know my work know many of my pictures are not living room decor. The fact that Jake had come surprised the hell out of me until he reminded me that I'd added him to my mailing list, back when...well...a while ago. But still, I couldn't fathom why he was here. He told me he'd wait for me so we could talk. As I chatted up pretty, affluent Bostonians, I fantasized about more than just chatting with Jake, but I was reasonably sure he was here for the big closure speech, maybe to buy a conciliatory piece as a gesture. I wouldn't let him though. He saved my fucking life. He could have anything. Everything.

But it was still grand to see him. One could never grow tired of even a glimpse of his face. And I found that I honestly hoped he was happy. That surprised me. But maybe it shouldn't have, for over the last few months I'd realized what was most important to me was that Jake was okay. After all, that was the bargain I'd made. I'd kept it. I'd made the deal in exchange for his life, and he did live, so... Rita said this was magical thinking. I replied that there was nothing wrong with magic and sang her a bunch of songs to prove it.

It was late and the gallery was emptying. While the assistant was busy talking to a patron, I indicated to her that I was done. With a jerk of my head, I signaled to Jake to follow me. The side door at the back of the space led to a hallway that bisected the building. We headed toward the opposite exit from the gallery entrance side. The Cathedral Station was not far away, so we headed there for a drink, sharing nothing on the walk over but banalities about the show. The anticipation of what Jake was going to say stirred up that little sea of sadness, but I'd listen, care, be happy for him, say goodbye. Easy as...yeah, fuck me.

The place was, perhaps, a little too noisy for an intimate conversation, but we found a quieter corner table. We ordered. I chose Glenlevit. Jake ordered a stout. While waiting, I asked Jake about his injury, how his recovery went.

"It's was surprisingly long," he said. "Even though I've known cops who got shot, I never really understood the process of recovery, you know? First, you have to regain the ability to sit up in bed, then stand, and then walk. It just weakens you. Even when you have the ability, you don't have the strength." He shook his head as if still in wonder. Then he looked up suddenly and said, "But you know that, Ian."

I smiled and was about to answer when the waiter brought our drinks. We sipped quietly for a moment. "Yeah," I said, remembering my long recovery. "It would have been a nightmare without someone to help me. I thank Arty for that anyway. I'm glad you had Chris there for you, Jake."

He gave me an odd look, with that tilted head thing that goes straight to my goddamn nuts. "Chris wasn't *there* for me, Ian. Had you bothered to return my call, you might have known that." Yeah, there was a little fire there.

I sat back, stunned. Although I didn't know why I should be. It was my chosen style: avoid the good by assuming the worst. "Jesus." I didn't have an immediate follow-up to that at the moment. We sat in silence for a long, long minute. I thought about what it might have meant had I returned the call. I imagined caring for this man, nursing, helping, atoning. But I'd made that bargain. "This is probably going to make you think I live on the edge of insanity. I probably do. But here's the thing: when I was kneeling on the sidewalk trying to hold your blood in—" The memory made the words catch, I admit. "—I made an agreement. Don't ask me with who: fate, God, Buddha, whatever. It was more of a question really: What do you want? Now, it sounds stupid. I thought then, if it meant you'd live, I'd give you up, never see you again. When you did live, I felt I had to fulfill a bargain. I didn't want to test it." *Christ. Run, Jake, run. This man is mad.* I shrugged my shoulders like the idiot I was. And honestly, I hadn't kept my bargain, strictly. I'd seen him twice in the hospital. "I saw him there—Chris. I assumed he'd take care of you. I imagined he would. That's how I got by. Believing he was there for you."

Jake sat quietly for a bit. Sipping at his stout, leaving a little creamy outline on his top lip that he'd lick away with the tip of his tongue, clearly not knowing what that was doing to me. "Well, rest easy, Ian. If you had returned my call, it wouldn't have been a call for help. Just a call to let you know I saw you at the hospital, and Chris wasn't there in any role but a friend. Really, the only reason he was there at all was because he was my emergency contact at the station. I forgot to change it after we split up." He sounded a little bitter, his voice tight. "I have family, you know. I didn't need you. Like that, I mean. To take care of me."

Sometimes my lack of vision astounds me. In all my musings had I ever thought about the kind of support Jake must have had from his huge family? I could have saved myself the struggle of imagining the intimacies that might have occurred in his caretaking. There are times that the parts of myself that I dislike race like an incoming tide up inlets of awareness and threaten to drown me. Right now, I was not liking my tendency to fill in blanks arbitrarily. No, not arbitrarily. I fill the unknown based on my insecurities, shame, self-loathing as if it were protection from those very feelings. Perhaps one day I'd learn to simply ask.

"To be honest, Ian. I didn't want anyone around much. It's not that I didn't think of continually calling you until you answered or called back. I just wanted to be healthier before I did. I mean, I don't think that starting something is a great idea when someone is in the middle of recovery."

"No, I suppose not," I responded, still lost in my thoughts. I caught up, though, and looked up at him. Jake was looking at me with those extraordinary blue eyes. I knew I would never tire of the spin I feel in my chest when I see them, like a child on his first elevator ride when the world goes out from under him. "Um, what are you saying, Jake?"

He smiled a shy smile which made him look boyish. "Well, I mean, I don't know what your current situation is, but if there's—"

"There's no one else, there's no *situation*. Where's your car?"

"In the lot by the gallery. Why?"

I stood, hung my cane on my arm, pulled my wallet out of my pocket, grabbed enough money for the tab and about three tips, took Jake by the arm, and hauled him out of the chair and into the night. "I have a hotel room nearby."

He laughed, grabbed me by my lapels, and kissed me. We cut through the park stopping from time to time to kiss and press our hardness against each other in the dark of a tree. As we neared the hotel, we instinctively parted a little, each chuckling as we let our arousal calm to a presentable state. Lucky that we were both wearing suits.

Once in the room, it was all on. I pushed Jake against the door by way of closing it with a very rude slam and shoved my body against his as I swept his arms above his head and held them with one hand. *This is right. This is good. This is where you belong.* Our mouths came together with a hook of the tip of his tongue. The sound of wet kisses—all about sex, all about how we can arouse, be aroused—filled the room. I ran my other hand along the inside of his suit jacket and pinched his nipple hard through the soft cotton of his shirt. He pushed his groin against me as I cupped his erection. We moved from the door and managed to strip between kisses as we made our way to the bed, the dim light of the entryway casting a warm glow.

I landed with a soft thump on my back. Jake stepped between my legs and bent over me. "I want to make love to you, Ian, to please you. Can we try this again?"

I wasn't sure whether he meant that he wanted to try the relationship again or the topping again, but it didn't matter—same answer. "Yes, sure, of course. I don't think—" he stopped my blathering with his mouth. Kissing and licking, he made his way to my nipple, making the tiny useless thing stand up at his bite while he tweaked the other one with his fingers. A deep rumble came from somewhere, and after a moment, I realized it was me. He moved his mouth to my cock and ran his tongue around the rim flicking at the underside a few times before taking the entirety into his mouth. I could only grab his hair and hold on. His machinations took me close, but he stopped short, letting loose with a soft pop. He got fully onto the bed, and I scooted up, still on my back. Jake knelt between my legs and slid his hand under my knee, lifting until it was bent, propped upright. Sliding his hand around, he followed with my other leg. Fully exposed, I felt salacious and deliciously nasty.

"Uh-oh," said Jake, "lube?" Fuck and damn.

"Shit. Bathroom. Lotion, conditioner, shampoo. I don't care. I have one condom." He made a beeline for the choices, and I grabbed my wallet where I knew there was an emergency condom. Back in position, Jake chose lotion. It had a pleasing flowery, citrusy scent. He rubbed it playfully around my nipple and trailed his finger down and down, hooking it under my balls to lift them slightly. He lubed two fingers with the chilly cream and positioned them at my entrance. He looked up and raised his eyebrows at me in question. I nodded go. Gently, he nudged me open with one finger and waited, then added the other when he felt a little give of the muscle. The sounds I made were spontaneous, animal groans and growls which Jake rewarded with comments like "Christ, that sound makes me nuts" and a few more detailed ones. He asked me questions; did it feel good? Did I like his fingers in my ass? The lewdness was erotic and delicious. He worked a rhythm for a while then turned his palm up. I knew he was checking my face for panic, I hope he saw what I was feeling; need, want, sex in its rawest form. He found the gland and my legs shuddered involuntarily. A quiet almost exclusively inner bounce in pleasure set in with his stroking. I uttered a continuous stream of "fuck" as I came close.

"I'm... Jake... I want you inside me. Hurry." He withdrew his fingers and ripped open the only condom, smoothed it on, lubed and was at the spot in seconds. He pushed cautiously at first and when he sensed that I was still open drove in. As he found our cadence, his liturgy of obscenity started. It was such a turn on that I came fast and hard, laughing out loud at myself... "Fuck's sake, don't stop. Harder, Jake. Fuck me harder." Later, I thought that feeling Jake fill me was much like finding my way through a painting, each starting, each thrust of brush or cock brought me closer to the answer, the last piece of the puzzle, the climax.

But the loud slapping of Jake's groin against my ass, his commentary, and my grunts and oaths, overwhelmed me and I felt myself starting to slip away, heading for another flashback.

When Jake put his mouth to my ear and said, "Your fucking ass is so tight; squeeze a little, Ian; Jesus Christ, that's sweet," I was back in the moment. God, I could come again listening, fascinated by his inventiveness. Then suddenly he was quiet, and I met his eyes; his wet lips were parted a little, gasping. He looked at me—no, it felt more like *into* me. Not the look of distraction that I'd seen before orgasm, but with an extraordinary focus. It was me he was coming into, *me*.

Later, after a perfunctory cleanup, we lay entwined, my head on his chest, his strong hot arms around me. The bed had double duvets, European style, that we'd long since shoved to the floor. For now, it was warm enough to lie naked next to each other. I bent my neck to look up at him and saw the scar of the bullet wound, and my throat tightened at the memories. "Jake, I've always wanted to thank you for saving my life." I stretched to kiss his neck at the entry point.

He looked over at me, his blue eyes iridescent. "Hey, you saved mine, too, Ian."

I wasn't sure either of us was talking about the shooting.

*

We dozed a little. Jake sat up abruptly and said, "This isn't going to work."

It said something that I didn't think he was talking about us. "What, love?"

He jumped out of bed and started to dress. Now I was a little antsy.

"Jake?"

"Once. Once is not going to work. I'm going to find condoms. There must be a CVS open around here. Check your phone."

He was back in my arms in less than twenty minutes.

One time that night our joining had a sense of desperation, a clinging to life, about it. A tenderness that seemed to express how close we had come to losing each other. But more often, the sex was joyful and lit with laughter and teasing. Early in the morning as I lay listening to Jake's gentle snore, wondering about a future, a line came to me, and then another, and one more. I rose quietly, not bothering with clothing and searched as silently as possible for pen and paper. Cracking the darkening drapes slightly, a sliver of streetlight shone on the table near the window. It was enough to write by. It was a rough start, many false ones, as I stretched a part of me that had been long dormant. I stopped often to watch Jake sleep loose and graceful, arm thrown over his head, legs akimbo.

By the time the sun started to rise, I was entirely into it, sucked back into the search for and arranging of words that had sustained me most of my adult life. At some point, I realized the quiet. Jake's soft purr had stopped. I looked over to see him watching me. He smiled.

"Good?" was his simple question.

I smiled back and nodded.

Two cerulean seas vivid rafts of emerald matrix
they are two fathoms deep
two times the depth of a man's
outstretched arms
to hold
to sink
to swim...

About the Author

Pamela A. Williams is a Clinical Social Worker living and working on the Southcoast of Massachusetts. She is the daughter John E. Williams, winner of the 1973 National Book Award for *Augustus*. She has always had writing in her blood but has only lately found the serenity and confidence to put pen to paper (or fingers to keyboard, if you will).

Ms. Williams comes from a widely varied background. She's worked in manufacturing, retail, graphic arts and the mental health field. She tries to bring these experiences to her writing to create well rounded, believable characters. And she remains forever honored and grateful to her clients who have shared their personal stories and broadened her view of humanity. She is awed by their resilience and trust.

She lives with two cats, of course.

Email: pwilliamswriter@gmail.com

Twitter: @PAWilliamsWord

Website: www.pawilliamsauthor.com